"I THOUGHT YOU SAID THIS WAS SAFE," GRAHAM murmured, his hands reaching under her sweater as they sat in his car in a corner of the deserted school lot.

"Dangerous," Elaine gasped out, her fingers tugging at his hair. "You make me feel so dangerous tonight."

"You make me feel like we've gone parking on a date. I'm all urges, and all for you."

"Too bad we can't," she murmured. "Because, Lord, how I want to."

Graham paused and raised his head from where he'd been nuzzling her neck. His expression was full of hopeful anticipation. "We're really not teenagers who've gone parking, and so we couldn't . . . or could we?"

She gazed back at him. "We're far too old to be behaving in such a scandalous manner."

He whispered something particularly scandalous in her ear, and she made a shocked noise.

"We shouldn't."

"We couldn't."

Her hands went to the buttons of her skirt.

He pushed his seat back. . . .

WHAT ARE *LOVESWEPT* ROMANCES?

They are stories of true romance and touching emotion. We believe those two very important ingredients are constants in our highly sensual and very believable stories in the LOVE-SWEPT line. Our goal is to give you, the reader, stories of consistently high quality that may sometimes make you laugh, sometimes make you cry, but are always fresh and creative and contain many delightful surprises within their pages.

Most romance fans read an enormous number of books. Those they truly love, they keep. Others may be traded with friends and soon forgotten. We hope that each LOVESWEPT romance will be a treasure—a "keeper." We will always try to publish

LOVE STORIES YOU'LL NEVER FORGET
BY AUTHORS YOU'LL ALWAYS REMEMBER

The Editors

Loveswept® 735

THE PERFECT CATCH

LINDA CAJIO

BANTAM BOOKS
NEW YORK · TORONTO · LONDON · SYDNEY · AUCKLAND

THE PERFECT CATCH

A Bantam Book / April 1995

LOVESWEPT *and the wave design are registered trademarks of*
Bantam Books, a division of Bantam Doubleday Dell Publishing Group,
Inc. Registered in U.S. Patent and Trademark Office and elsewhere.

All rights reserved.
Copyright © 1995 by Linda Cajio.
Back cover art copyright © 1995 by Barney Plotkin.
Floral border by Lori Nelson Field.
No part of this book may be reproduced or transmitted in any
form or by any means, electronic or mechanical,
including photocopying, recording, or by any
information storage and retrieval system, without
permission in writing from the publisher.
For information address: Bantam Books.

If you would be interested in receiving protective vinyl covers for your
Loveswept books, please write to this address for information:

Loveswept
Bantam Books
P.O. Box 985
Hicksville, NY 11802

ISBN 0-553-44507-3

Published simultaneously in the United States and Canada

Bantam Books are published by Bantam Books, a division of Bantam Dou-
bleday Dell Publishing Group, Inc. Its trademark, consisting of the words
"Bantam Books" and the portrayal of a rooster, is Registered in U.S. Patent
and Trademark Office and in other countries. Marca Registrada. Bantam
Books, 1540 Broadway, New York, New York 10036.

PRINTED IN THE UNITED STATES OF AMERICA

OPM   0 9 8 7 6 5 4 3 2 1

Many thanks to the 1993 Boys of Summer who gave Philadelphia its "Enchanted Season" and who gave back to me my long-dormant love of the game. The nice part about being a writer is that I get to write it my way, so for those in the know . . . you'll know.

This book is for my grandmother and my aunts, baseball lovers all.

ONE

"Whoooo! Struck him out, the stinkin' loser!"

Elaine Sampson clamped her hand over her mouth and flopped back into her seat, horrified at her outburst. It didn't matter that the crowd at Veterans Stadium was roaring its own approval as the Atlanta Braves batter walked away dejected from the plate, struck out by Philadelphia Phillies pitcher Curt Schilling.

"Mom!" her son, Anthony, exclaimed, staring at her with a thirteen-year-old's complete mortification for his mother's embarrassing action. His face was bright red as he glanced around to see if anyone was looking.

"Hot damn! Leave her be, sugar," Cleo Burfield said to Anthony. The big black woman patted him on the back in commiseration. "First home game of the season and your mama's ready for action."

Anthony grinned at Cleo. If Cleo approved, it was cool.

"Never thought I'd hear *that* from you, Elaine," Mary Ososa said, pressing her rosary beads one after the other in silent prayer as the next batter faced Schilling. Mary was as prim as Cleo was sassy, although she was grinning at Elaine.

"It's about time we heard that from her, Mary," Jean Keenan said, laughing. "We've been the Widows' Club for nearly two years now, and she's never lost it before at a game."

"I've got to stop listening to the morning guys on WIP radio," Elaine muttered, slouching down in her seat. She still couldn't believe she had shouted like a fishwife. Her, a seventh-grade schoolteacher with a master's degree, for goodness sake. But the Phils were the Phils. They *had* to win their home opener.

The two men in the row in front of her had turned around at her outburst, and she realized they were still staring at her. Their more formal clothes gave them away as businessmen attending the game, probably in their company's block of seats, a business entertainment phenomenon of the last few years. "Suits," the fans called the corporate types, because they just sat and did deals, barely watching the game. Certainly they never cheered for the team, either team. They never clapped for a player. And they *always* left before the eighth inning, to beat the inevitable traffic jam. Even worse, by getting season tickets to choice seats, they moved more fans to the upper levels of the stadium, out of the lower 100, 200, and 300 levels. Elaine felt lucky her little crowd still managed to get in their same 300-level row year after year when they bought their own season tickets.

One of the men in front of her, with the perfect hair pulled back in a tiny male ponytail, and with the perfect tan, *and* with a pierced hoop earring in one ear, glared up at her as if she had uttered absolute filth at him. She knew he was thinking she was one of "those" kinds of fans, abusive and without manners in general. The other man, although wearing an expensive suit and also sporting a perfect, if shorter, haircut, looked less urban-plastic than his companion. He was older, for one thing— around forty, she judged. His face was lean and rugged, with age lines beginning around the mouth. His hair was dark except for a few silver strands at his temples, just one or two, as if he'd earned them early rather than through the normal aging process. Elaine had noticed him before, when he had sat down. Throughout the opening innings, she had found herself catching glimpses of his profile, which had somehow piqued her curiosity and made her wish she could get a full look at him.

Her wish had now come true. As the man stared at her, her heart beat at lightning speed, her tongue stuck to the roof of her mouth, and her brain turned to complete mush. But her insides were swirling with a deliciously warm sensation that left her breathless. The intensity scared her, for she hadn't felt like this in a long, long time.

His eyes held her own gaze. They were a deep brown, the same color as the eyes of a fawn she had once nursed to adulthood. Gentleness, though, wasn't in the depths of these eyes. They were hard-edged . . . speculating . . . impossible to turn from.

Panic shot through Elaine as if she'd just found herself teetering on the edge of a cliff. The noise of the crowd faded to a vague mumble until the world seemed to darken and close in around her and the man. He glanced lower, his gaze traveling down and back up again, taking in her red Phillies cap with her ponytail poking through the gap in the back, her hooded sweatshirt, jeans, thick white crew socks, and sneakers. He couldn't see much of her body, not with the way she was huddled in the molded plastic seat. But every inch of her felt the shock of his gaze. Here she was, a thirty-seven-year-old widow with one adolescent son, and she couldn't remember the last time a man had looked at her like this. She ought to be flattered, but she felt as vulnerable as a rabbit under a wolf's paw. She also wished she was ten pounds slimmer and in a strapless gown. Heck, this kind of male assessment came along once in a blue moon, and she ought to look good when it did.

"Mom . . . Mom!"

The man turned forward again, finally breaking

their locked gazes. Elaine blinked. She took a deep, cleansing breath, trying to regain her equilibrium. The world came back into focus.

The bright lights of the Vet blazed down on the field, illuminating the players. The crowd's cheers were suddenly deafening, the salty odor of popcorn and the sweet scent of soda overpowering. People all around her were on their feet, screaming at the top of their lungs.

Curt had struck out another one.

She grinned at her son, who was cheering and hugging Cleo. She knew he would die a thousand deaths before he hugged his own mother in public. Cleo was different.

"Bottom of the fourth, and my boy's coming up!" Cleo announced proudly.

"If Lenny Dykstra really was your boy, we'd have the story of the year," Jean said, chuckling. She was tall and angular where Cleo was short and busty.

"I couldn't be his mama!" Cleo laughed with glee. "Lenny's Mr. Excitement. Whenever he's at bat, he gives me that sexual high." She belatedly put her hands over Anthony's ears. "You cover your ears, baby, you're not near ready for this. But, oh my, if my Luther were still alive, I'd be saying 'Get ready, Luther, tonight's your lucky night!' "

The three older widows erupted into laughter. Anthony grinned. Elaine, normally used to this banter, found her face turning red because of the man in front of her.

"You hush up and watch, Jean," Cleo added. "We're down one run, and Lenny is about to tie it up."

"He better," Mary muttered, the beads moving through her fingers at record speed. "If someone doesn't break this game open soon, those you-know-what Braves are going to win."

It was odd how she had come together with these women, all of whom were in their sixties, Elaine thought. They had met years ago right here in this row, when Anthony had been little. She hadn't had an interest in the game at the time; she'd come for her husband's sake. But they had become friendly with their seat "neighbors." Mary's husband had already passed on after a long illness, so Elaine had never met him. Jean's husband had died from a stroke the year after they'd met, and four years back Luther's heart had given out suddenly.

And then her own husband, Joe, had died, long before he should have. It had happened a little over a year and a half ago. Joe had gone out for bread and milk, and someone had run a red light on Route 70 when Joe had been crossing. She had been left with a house with a too big mortgage payment, a young son, and little insurance.

The women had been staunch support then, and she often felt she had been blessed with three extra mothers. Cleo, Jean, and Mary hadn't given up their season tickets after their husbands' deaths because they were true aficionados of baseball.

Elaine had continued going to the games for Anthony at first, because the boy needed men to look up to, men who could show him man things, who could show him that hard work and dedication paid off. A baseball team he had idolized all his short life seemed a good place to start. She had had to learn the finer points of the game for her son's sake, and slowly she'd become a true fan.

Jean had started calling them the Widows' Club, and Elaine had evolved into a chauffeur for them all. With this season opener at the Vet, she sensed something big about to happen with the team, and it had infected her. Baseball. Springtime with the all-American pastime. Somehow the combination had pushed itself into her soul, and at that moment, nothing was finer.

It had to be the game, she told herself, because it couldn't be the man in front of her.

To her horror, Cleo leaned over and tapped both "suits" on the shoulder. "You boys better be watching this, or you'll miss the play of the game."

"But he's down two strikes already!" the younger man said in disbelief to Cleo.

Cleo sniffed. "That's just part of Lenny's show. He'll work that count to a full one and make that pitcher throw ten times, just trying to get him out. Wears those snotty pitcher boys down and gets them off the mound early."

"Here endeth the lesson of the day," Mary said.

"Amen to that!" Jean added.

Elaine looked for heavenly salvation herself,

because mortification of the flesh was already guaranteed. Those three were in rare form tonight.

The younger man made a face. The older one just shook his head. Elaine resisted the urge to dump her soda all over them. Cleo was only being friendly, which was more than she could say for those two—even if one was sexy as hell.

The tension in the stadium built to a fever pitch as Lenny Dykstra sent several pitches foul into the stands and passed on a few more, until his count was three balls and two strikes, just as Cleo had predicted. A few more pitches went foul as Mr. Excitement lived up to his name. Elaine forgot about the man sitting in front of her. She forgot about "suits" in general . . . and her name, her job, and other vital pieces of information as her exhilaration level built with each pitch. She squeezed her soda cup, threatening to overflow the contents, grabbed Jean's hand with her free one, and thought her heart would burst through her chest as she waited for each windup and pitch. It was going to happen, she thought, feeling the truth of it in her bones.

The Sure Thing.

She suddenly understood Cleo's need for Luther, because her whole body was thrumming with anticipation, her blood whirling hot along her veins. She was desperate for something to relieve the growing sensuality . . . for someone . . .

Her gaze dropped to the disturbing man in front of her. To her shock, he turned around at that very moment as if her body had called to his. If his first stare had sent her spiraling, this one catapulted her into dizzying heights as her body responded to the physical attraction she felt toward this man. She couldn't look away, couldn't focus on anything but him.

The man broke the gaze as the smack of wood against leather was heard over the stadium roar, as a ball was hit with tremendous force. Elaine looked up in time to see the little white ball sailing back . . . back . . . The outfielder ran to the warning track . . . his arm was outstretched . . . he jumped right at the wall . . .

The ball sailed over the right-field fence into the Phillies bull pen. A home run.

Elaine screamed and leaped to her feet, flinging her arms up with joy. Just as she did, she realized she was still holding her soda cup, and the soda inside was taking a leap of its own. She watched in fascinated horror as it moved in almost slow-motion time out of the cup and into the air, the dark liquid spreading out in a kind of wall twinkling with crushed ice. The soda hit the man in front of her with a solid splash, and the world, which had been frozen for that one terrible instant, suddenly returned again in all its loud noisy glory.

The man yelped and jumped to his feet, soda dripping down his head and the back of his suit jacket.

"Omigod, omigod!" Elaine exclaimed, grabbing up her napkins and rubbing at his hair and back. She could feel her face heating with embarrassment and wondered if she was getting psychic in her old age. "I'm so sorry. I'm so sorry!"

He pushed her hands away as she rubbed the already soaked napkins to shreds. People around them were laughing and cheering, half for the batter jogging around the bases and half for the entertainment she had just provided. Her three female companions were roaring with laughter. Even her son was giggling.

"I'm so sorry," she said to the man. Her face was burning now. "I feel awful. I'll go with you to the rest room, where I can sponge the soda off."

"You don't put water on an Italian silk suit, you stupid idiot!" the younger man yelped, waving his hands. "I can't believe you ignoramuses here. They ought to charge more for seats so we get a better class of people at the games."

"Shut up!" Anthony burst out, stepping in front of Elaine as if to protect her. "That's my mother and it was an accident!"

Tears sprang to Elaine's eyes at her son's action. She forced them away, knowing he'd be humiliated if she started to cry because she was proud of him.

"The boy's right, it was an accident," the older man said. To Anthony he added, "I'm sorry for what Ed said. Don't worry about what happened."

Ed looked about ready to swallow his teeth, every pearly one of them. "But, Graham . . ." He stopped and turned to Elaine, a look of disgust on his face. "I'm sorry."

Elaine said nothing to him, wishing she could crawl into a hole. Anthony, too, had been made to look childlike with the adult interference.

"Thanks, Anthony." She squeezed his shoulders gratefully. Her son was her height now, a fact that brought itself home to her in a poignant way even in this weird situation.

An usher showed up at the commotion, and the man Graham explained that some soda had been spilled, no problem. The usher left and people began to sit down again.

"Please," she said to the man before he turned away. "At least let me have your suit dry-cleaned for you."

"No. That's all right." He sat down, his back to her.

She couldn't blame him. Cleo sniffed, while Jean made a face. Mary's rosary clacked. Elaine took a deep breath and tapped him on the shoulder. He turned, staring at her.

"Really, I want to make amends," she said. "Let me take care of this for you."

He shook his head and turned back.

She reached into her hip pack and took out a twenty. She tapped the man on the shoulder again. He whipped around. She waved the money in his face. "Here. This should cover it."

The younger man snorted, clearly indicating that what she offered was far short of the price the cleaning would cost. Elaine wondered just how much one paid for an Italian silk suit to be cleaned.

Did the silk from Italy have some special property that defied normal dry-cleaning methods?

"Thanks for the offer," Graham said, "but I can take care of my own dry cleaning."

His voice wasn't unpleasant, she mused. In fact, it sent a slight chill down her spine that had nothing to do with the April night air.

"No. I insist."

"Lady, look, it's not necessary."

"It is." But short of stuffing the money into his pocket—and that thought made her fingers tremble—she didn't know what else to do. Then an idea occurred to her. She dug into her hip pack again, while saying, "I have a friend who owns a dry cleaners in Malvern. She can handle your suit, I'm sure. She does a lot of executives out that way. Here's her address." She finally dug out one of the business cards she carried for her friend's establishment. Taking the pen Jean was using to keep score and ignoring her squawks at being robbed, Elaine scribbled on the back of the card before holding it out to him. "Nancy owes me a favor, so she'll be glad to do your suit for you. I'll call her tomorrow and let her know. The address and phone number are on the card, and I put my address and phone number on the back in case you have a problem, but you shouldn't. Really, I wouldn't feel right if I didn't take care of your suit for you. Please let me do this."

The man stared at her for the longest moment. Elaine had an awful feeling she'd just grown a second head. He had a great ability to skewer people with his gaze, she thought. So had Dracula. And just like Dracula, he exuded a subtle sensuality. She could feel it swirling through her, as if he were actually undressing her. More years than she cared to count had passed since the last time she'd felt this way with a man. Other women could handle themselves sexually, but after fourteen years of marriage she was out of practice. *Way* out. And the game was so different at thirty-seven than it had been at twenty.

She shoved the card at him to break the trance. He took it reluctantly.

She smiled in relief. "Nancy does nice work. You won't be sorry, I promise."

He turned forward at last. Elaine slumped in her chair, feeling as if she'd just been let out of prison. She resisted the urge to fan herself. Poise was a better defense.

Opening day was full of surprises, she thought, and not all of them with the team.

Graham Reed sat in misery. Cold soda had wormed its way under his jacket and shirt, chilling his skin. The cool night air didn't help. Worse, the liquid left a sticky feeling on his scalp and neck. He, a basketball man, was at a baseball game, a sport for the unskilled as far as he was concerned. Ed Tarksas squeezed him in on his right, and a complete stranger continually rubbed against him on the left.

And behind him sat a beautiful maniac.

Maybe "beautiful" wasn't the right word, he thought. He had been aware of the woman sitting behind him ever since he'd taken his seat, but hadn't bothered to turn around until her screaming outburst. And then he hadn't been able to look away.

She wore a Phillies baseball cap low on her forehead, and the way her ponytail swept along her shoulders, curling just at the ends, so dark in color it was almost black, reminded him of a young girl's. His fingers had ached to touch it, to feel it twine around his hand with its own vitality. Large hoop earrings of thin gold hung elegantly from her ears, combining with the cap for an incongruous look that somehow worked on her. Her face wasn't model thin, yet her cheekbones were noticeable and her skin was smooth, creamy, with a touch of color from the night's chill. Her lips were full, intriguing, and he'd found himself wanting to taste them, to see if they would meld perfectly with his. Her figure was covered up in a sweatshirt jacket and jeans, but he could tell it was an attractive one. He judged her to be in her mid-thirties, a time in life that gave her maturity and experience . . . and a latent sensuality. He could sense it, he could see it, and he felt as if he'd been walloped by a two-by-four just from looking at her.

The boy alongside her was enough like her in

coloring and features to mark him as her son. And although he didn't need anyone to pay for his dry cleaning, he had to admit he liked her insistence on making amends. That said a lot about her as a person. And he liked the way the boy had come to her defense. She had stared him down, and stared down Ed, so she was hardly in need of any defending, but the child's gesture said a lot about her as a parent.

Still, a child. He and children didn't mix well, so he avoided women who had them. Of course, it didn't matter in this case; she had to be married.

A trickle of melted ice made its way under his shirt and trailed along his shoulder. Graham adjusted his shirt collar and pushed at the wetness, trying in vain to shift it off his body. The wet stickiness around his neck was suddenly unbearable, so he got up and went to the men's room on the concourse below.

The room's cleanliness surprised him, and nobody did more than glance at him as he stripped off his suit jacket and shirt, then rinsed off his hair and shoulders as best he could in one of the sinks. The air was cool inside the building, swirling around his bare arms and chest and raising goosebumps. He toweled off with paper towels, then pushed the electric hand dryer on and held his wet clothes under its already hot nozzle. He frowned as the dark stain grew more pronounced as the clothes dried. His maniac had nailed him good. . . .

"Excuse me."

Men standing in front of the open urinals yelped at the female voice coming from the doorway and began frantically adjusting clothing. Graham started and whirled around. His maniac was standing in the open doorway as if he'd conjured her up. The two-by-four hit again, with even more force.

She was half turned away, averting her gaze, but that didn't stop the consternation caused by a woman on the edge of invading the last of male refuges on the planet. Neither did it stop Graham from suddenly feeling too warm and too conscious of her presence. She looked even better standing up than she did sitting down. Way better . . .

"If you dry it without washing the stain out first, it may set," she advised.

He found his voice—and his reason. "Are you crazy? This is *the men's room!*"

Men bleated in horror behind him, like a Greek chorus, and that seemed to move her finally. She dipped out of sight behind the outer modesty wall. The men subsided, but they glared at him as if he were at fault for the near breach.

"I'm sorry," she called out. It seemed her voice wasn't disappearing. "But I got worried when you were picking at your collar and then left. I thought I better check and see if I could help. Do you want me to take it and wash it in the ladies' room?"

"No thanks," he said quickly, having a vision of himself standing outside the ladies' room half naked. He shoved his clothes under the still-running dryer, muttering, "Come on, come on . . ."

"I forgot that getting silk wet was bad. Are you drying it again? You shouldn't."

"I'll take my chances," he said, wondering what she'd thought when she'd looked in and caught him topless. Probably that he ought to be ten pounds thinner and work out regularly, he decided, then wondered what the hell he was doing wondering. His chest was acquiring a gray hair or two, as well, among the dark brown . . .

"I'm Elaine Sampson, by the way. You're Graham, right?"

He blinked in confusion and answered automatically, "Yes. Graham Reed."

"Nice name."

There was a long silence. Graham could think of nothing to say, so he said, "Thanks."

"I hope you'll take me up on my offer, especially now if the stain's set. You'll really need a good dry cleaner. I'm a widow, and I have a young son. You saw him . . ."

Her voice trailed away and he realized he needed to answer. "Yes, I did."

"With his father gone, it's doubly important for me to set a good example for him. Are you a parent?"

Heads turned. Graham swallowed and said to no one in particular, "She spilled soda on my suit."

"What did you say?"

"No, I'm not a parent, not even married," he

called out. "Could we have this conversation later?"

"Yeah," a guy in a stall yelled. "Could we have this conversation later?"

"Oh. Yes, of course, but if I don't fix your suit, then he'll think it's okay not to fix things he's damaged."

"Lady, I do understand and admire that," Graham began, shaking his jacket and shirt to quicken the drying process. The dryer turned off in a complete lack of cooperation. He slapped the start button, then realized he might have better luck if he put the shirt *outside* the jacket, rather than have it tucked inside because it was easier to hold. He switched it around, cursing himself for being seduced into accepting Ed Tarksas's invitation to the ball game, just so he could listen to the man's advertising campaign pitch for Graham's chain of pizzerias. Cove Pizzerias couldn't afford the slick TV, radio, and print ads Ed wanted to blanket over the Delaware Valley. Graham only owned twenty places in the state of Delaware, the most profitable in the coastal resort towns, so he wasn't sure a huge campaign would be cost-effective, despite Ed's intense sales pitch all during the game.

Now Graham wasn't thinking about anything other than this woman who wouldn't leave him to set his soda stain in peace. If she wanted to talk, he could think of better, more intimate places . . .

"Then you'll go to have your suit cleaned?"

"If I don't hang myself first," he muttered.

"What did you say?"

"Nothing!" he shouted, wondering if she could read thoughts. Now, that was scary.

He heard a commotion outside, a boy shrieking and a woman's voice raised in annoyance. Now what was she doing? Mugging kids?

"What are you doing?" he called out, feeling his shirt. It was definitely drying.

"Just a minute. We have a rebellion going on out here . . ." To someone else, she said, "I don't know this man who's in there at all, really, but I spilled soda on him and he was nice about it. Maybe he can watch your son. Mr. Reed?" Her voice rose again. "There's a little boy coming in to use the rest room. Could you keep an eye on him for his mother?"

Graham looked down at his bare chest, looked at the men milling around and who were looking at him as if he'd been swallowing flaming swords. He felt as if he were in a nightmare that would never end. Face it, Reed, he thought, it couldn't get any more bizarre.

"Uhh . . . send him in."

A boy of about five or six walked into the bathroom, too young for the men's room alone but too old for the ladies' room with Mom. The kid looked sullen and Graham couldn't blame him. He smiled at the boy encouragingly, saying, "Moms are right to be concerned, but they don't understand, do they?"

The boy didn't answer, just went about his

business with quick efficiency while the other men grinned at him. Graham sighed, seeing the usual result of whenever he tried to be friendly with a child. Kids didn't like him. He was uncomfortable around them, he always had been. On the rare occasions he had familial and paternal stirrings, he put them aside, knowing his business took all his time and knowing he wouldn't be a very good parent.

The boy headed for the exit door on the opposite side of the rest room, and Graham called out dutifully, "Okay, he's coming out now."

The boy turned and stuck his tongue out at Graham. Several of the men chuckled. Compounded evidence on his incompetency with kids, Graham thought.

He put on his shirt, not caring that it still had a damp spot or two. After buttoning it, he finally left the men's room. The jacket he'd live with. It was only damp now, at least, rather than soaked.

Elaine was still waiting for him out on the busy concourse. She smiled at him, and although the mother and the boy were gone, she said, "Thanks. That was nice of you. The boy refused to go into the ladies' room with his mother and threw a tantrum about it."

"I don't think he was too happy with the compromise," Graham said, smiling ruefully. "He stuck his tongue out at me."

She shook her head. "Kids. Still, public rest rooms are a problem when you're a mom out alone with your son. Anthony was about the same age when he insisted he was old enough to use the men's room. How's the shirt and jacket?"

"Dry enough."

"I feel really bad about spilling soda on you."

"Don't." He grinned. "Actually, it was an adventure."

As she smiled back, he had an odd urge to reach for her and kiss her. Her smile faded, as if she sensed the attraction he felt for her.

"This is trouble," she said in a low voice.

"I'm not trouble," he assured her, feeling suddenly dangerous and impulsive, two sensations he never had.

"Yes, you are," she said. "You have eyes like a little deer I raised when I was a kid and lived in upstate Pennsylvania. But yours are . . ."

"Are what?" He had to know. He was thirty-seven years old, and he had to know.

"Are more intense," she finished.

She didn't know what intense was, he thought. The way she was looking at him shook him down to his feet. That was intense.

Someone bumped into him, and he realized they were standing in the concourse, traffic traveling around them. The physical attraction snapped off as if by a switch, and he immediately felt awkward, like a schoolboy talking with a girl for the first time.

"Ah, I better get back up there," Elaine said.

He nodded. "Me too."

"I'll get fries to cover my tracks." She smiled slightly as she began walking over to the nearest concession stand.

He followed her. "Why do you have to cover your tracks?"

"Because my friends are nosy and my son usually is mortified by me. He's thirteen. Kids embarrass easily at that age."

"Oh."

She got her fries in a large cup. She offered them to him, and because they smelled good and salty, he took one. It was fat and long—and hot.

"There goes the cholesterol, right through the roof," she quipped, before taking a bite of one herself.

The fry tasted as good as it smelled, the salt melting in his mouth. He grinned at her. "They're good."

"The best." She cleared her throat. "Maybe you want to go up ahead of me. Otherwise they'll think I've been nagging you and will tease me."

"And your son will be mortified."

"Because he thinks I'm a nag too. I'm actually a worrier. Really, though, use my friend for your suit. She'll do a good job, and I'll feel better."

"I suppose if I don't, you'll spill french fries down it." The card she'd given him was burning a hole in his jacket pocket. That he wasn't wearing the jacket at the moment didn't matter. He knew the card was there, like a lure.

She laughed. He couldn't remember the last

time he'd made a woman laugh. He liked the sound of hers. He liked the nagging. Or worrying. He couldn't remember the last time a woman had worried over him, either. It was nice.

He left her on the concourse, reluctantly, but with a small smile as he entered the stadium proper. He slipped on his slightly damp jacket and climbed the concrete steps to his seat. The small contingent above him, he saw, noticed him immediately. He realized he still had no idea who these three older women were and what their relationship was to Elaine Sampson. Nice name, he thought. Her son glanced at him, then looked back to the action taking place on the diamond. She was setting a fine example, he thought, because the boy seemed well mannered. He wondered what the father had been like.

He settled down next to Ed again. "Did I miss anything?"

"Just another homer, honey," came a voice behind him.

He turned slightly to see the black woman better. She was grinning knowingly at him. "Thanks."

He turned back around in time to see Elaine stroll out of the concourse entrance. She was munching on her french fries as innocently as any teenager. And she looked so damn good.

"She bought french fries!"

Howls of indignation went up behind him, along with vows to make Elaine share her goodies.

Graham found himself smiling smugly. He'd gotten one first, when it was still hot.

All of a sudden he heard a loud smack. The crowd was up and screaming. Graham stood more out of curiosity than interest. Another home run by one of the Phillies. He had to say the team was giving the fans their money's worth tonight.

He glanced over some heads to the aisle, expecting to see Elaine still making her way up the stairs. Instead, to his astonishment, she was standing in the middle of the aisle, next to a stranger, doing some kind of dance.

As her hips rocked from side to side, she pointed her forefinger above her head, then brought it down diagonally across her body and up again, in counterpoint to her swaying hips. She did it with such abandonment that all kinds of images rocked through his brain, most of them requiring two bodies in a horizontal position. The people all around him started chanting, "Whoomp! There it is!" over and over as they did the same strange dance as Elaine.

She was like no other mother he had ever known. Somehow she had roused an entire group into whatever ritual they were doing, and she hadn't spilled one french fry in the process.

He liked her for that too.

Elaine knew exactly the moment when Graham Reed and his companion "suit" had left at the start of the eighth inning. It was as if a hard wall suddenly crumbled around her. She didn't know why she was disappointed that he hadn't stayed for the end of the game, nor did she understand why she had pushed so hard for him to take advantage of her offer. It was true that she needed to ensure Anthony learned to correct his mistakes and treat other people's property with respect, but maybe she'd been too extreme this time.

More important, Graham Reed was dangerous. He was too sophisticated for her, too smooth, too corporate. Even in the rest room he'd been composed, never showing anything beyond initially being startled. And afterward, when they'd stood together on the concourse . . .

She wasn't ready to think seriously about men again. Granted, there hadn't been anyone about whom she could think seriously. Bill Voss, who taught eighth-grade math, was single and nice, yet he had never caused a ripple of attraction in her. But this Graham Reed, he could light fires without moving a muscle. That sort of man didn't instill notions of stability in a woman. Elaine told herself she should be grateful he thought she was a klutzy nut.

"Strike three!" Cleo shouted. The fans roared to their feet as the last out of the top of the ninth inning was made. The Phillies had won. Elaine's attention went back to where it belonged.

She rose, applauding with the rest of the members of the Widows' Club.

TWO

"Anthony! You forgot to take up your laundry!" Elaine shouted up the stairs while she eyed a pile of perfectly folded jeans and T-shirts.

"Aw, Mom!"

"Aw, Mom, nothing," she retorted firmly. "If you want to go out after dinner, then you better get on the stick now. And don't forget to put your things in your dresser drawers!"

She ignored the grumbling heard from above and went back into the kitchen to start another load of wash. On the way, she gave an affectionate pat to their cat, Mikey, where he lay on the sofa. Where was that good intention, she wondered, of not allowing the cat on the furniture? It had gone right out the window with a lot of other good intentions.

The kitchen radio blared the WIP sports talk show, getting people ready for the away game that night. The Phillies were on the road, so she was trying to catch up and get ahead on things before the team returned and the home games started again.

Really, she thought, surveying the mess in the middle of her kitchen floor, another good intention gone awry. Why couldn't she afford something better than a town house with the washer and dryer in the kitchen? Even a town house with a separate laundry room. Or, blessing of blessings, a home that had a basement?

"Because every extra room is an extra fifty-thou on a house. And I don't have one fifty-thou, let alone extras," she said out loud while lifting the sausage for her spaghetti sauce out of the frying pan to drain. Although they'd already eaten dinner, she'd decided to take advantage of the night off from both schoolwork and ball games to make several extra dinners to freeze for later. Another good intention that was giving her a doubly busy night.

Besides, the problem wasn't so much the small house, but her super busy schedule of work, home life, and ball games on an average of four nights out of seven. It would be like this until June, she thought ruefully, until she was done teaching and had the summer off. Not working then made things tougher financially, but being a schoolteacher meant she was home with her son, something she felt was more important right now than avoiding the financial edge.

She wondered if Graham Reed would be at the

game again when the team got back from their
road trip, then she shivered, remembering that moment when she'd thought he was going to kiss her,
right on the concourse. But that was silly. Why
would he have any interest in her, a nearly middle-
aged woman with a child and a nearly middle-aged
spread? A man like him wasn't for her even if she
were interested, which she wasn't. Definitely, absolutely wasn't.

She drained off the pan's sausage drippings,
then pushed the chopped green peppers and onions
from a cutting board into the pan to sauté them.
They sizzled as they hit the hot pan, immediately
giving off an aromatic bouquet. Satisfied the vege-
tables were well on their way to cooking, she pulled
laundry from the washer and put it in the dryer.

It seemed he had the same idea about her anyway, she admitted, her thoughts going back to the
disturbing Graham Reed. She'd dumped her soda
on him nearly a week ago, yet Nancy, her dry
cleaner friend, had told her he'd never called or
stopped in. She thought he would have done that at
least.

She smiled, remembering his willingness to
watch over a little boy in the men's room. That had
been nice. And his ruefulness afterward when the
child had been unappreciative. She couldn't help
smiling as she thought of it. Her smile faded,
though, as she decided he wasn't taking her up on
her offer after all. She wasn't sure whether she
should be disappointed or not about that.

"Not disappointed," she said firmly, picking up a load of underwear as the next batch for the washer.

"Talking to yourself again?"

She straightened and looked at her son, who was standing at the kitchen entrance. She grinned. "Yes, I am. It's insanity. You get it from your kids. Did you take your clothes upstairs and put them away?"

He rolled his eyes. "Yes."

"There will be a clothes check later. Remember, I'm cleaning tomorrow night."

"I'll pass inspection."

"A miracle."

"Funny, Mom. Can I go to Steven's now?"

"Homework all done?"

"Yes."

"Be home by nine. It's a school night."

"Okay." He raced down the short hallway to the door. Elaine heard it open and hoped he would remember to shut it behind him. She didn't care to heat the outside, although that had been a lost cause since Anthony was old enough to open doors. Kids, for some reason, never shut doors on cold days and *always* shut them on beautiful days. A parent couldn't win.

"Hey, Mom! That guy is here, and I'm gone!"

Elaine frowned and walked to the hallway instead of to the washer, to see what Anthony was talking about. "What guy is here?"

The question was answered by Graham Reed

himself. He filled her front doorway, looking far too devastating in another expensive suit. She couldn't imagine how his silk shirt could be any whiter, his burgundy striped tie any richer, or his features any more commanding. What she did know was that she was wearing her old faded, torn sweats and no makeup, her hair was in a lopsided ponytail that was threatening to undo itself at any moment, and she was holding an armload of underwear. Male underwear.

Why was he here? Did this mean that maybe . . . Naaa, she thought.

Her face heated to near frying point with her shame at being caught like this. She was doomed to look like an idiot with this man. Her son was nowhere to be seen, already well on his way to Steven's house and leaving her alone with Graham Reed.

"Hello," he said. "Remember me?"

"Yes, of course. The man from the ball game." Her heart was pounding double time in an anticipation she couldn't define. What was he doing here? Somehow she didn't want to ask the question.

He smiled and answered it for her. "I was on my way to an appointment in Cherry Hill and thought I would bring you my suit to be cleaned. You were very persuasive about it. Have I come at a bad time?"

"No, oh, no."

Silence ensued. She realized she was standing in

the hallway with dirty underwear in her arms. She thought about the condition of her kitchen, yet knew her living room wasn't in better shape. Simple straightening up also went by the wayside every April through June, and the house needed more than straightening. In the kitchen the radio was blasting another not-too-bright opinion from a caller that the Phillies should trade Daulton, the star catcher, before his knees gave out altogether. At another time, Elaine might have muttered her own opinion that the team should start training the man in a year or two to be a first baseman, to extend his playing years and keep him in the lineup because Daulton was a hundred-runs-batted-in hitter. Instead she felt her face heat at what seemed like another intrusion into all-male territory. She still felt as if a sports talk radio station were forbidden fruit for her.

"Please come into the kitchen," she said, wondering why she should feel embarrassed because she was listening to the radio. Graham Reed caused all kinds of odd sensations within her that made no sense at all. "Don't mind the mess. I'm trying to catch up on laundry and future meals tonight."

He followed her into the room. It looked worse than she ever imagined it could, with piles of laundry all over the floor and the place smelling like a sub shop. Why couldn't he have come when she was dressed to pose for *Vogue* and her house was ready for the next cover of *House Beautiful*? Not that she or the house ever would be, but she could dream.

She switched off the radio, toning down the noise competition to sizzling food and dull dryer roaring. Realizing she was still holding the underwear, she dumped the load into the washer and switched on the dials, adding again to the noise level. She turned around and said over the sound of water rushing into the laundry tub, "Sit down."

He did sit, although he looked at her chair as if checking for moss. Her house wasn't *that* bad, she thought.

"Would you like coffee?" she asked. "I have some."

He looked at her hands that had just been full of dirty underwear, as if the suggestion of coffee poured by her was more terrible than Frankenstein's monster coming to life. She wished she could dump herself into the washer and come out looking like a decent human being instead of the schlubb from hell—and acting like one too.

"No, thanks." He smiled. "I only have a minute."

He looked even more elegant and expensive in her kitchen—and more out of place than ever. And good-looking, she had to admit. The suit rested perfectly on his broad shoulders and tapered down past narrow male hips. If he had any fat on him, it didn't show. She knew. She'd had a good glimpse of him in that rest room. Lord, she thought as her blood rushed to her face again, this time from something entirely different than embarrassment. He was solidly built, with a covering of dark hair on his chest. She wondered if he worked out regularly, for she'd seen well-defined arms.

Cleo would probably say he got her motor running. Elaine felt like hers was in third gear already, revving fast with the warmth that was shooting through her veins at his presence. She took a deep breath to try to control her body, more conscious than ever of her working clothes and the extra ten pounds hanging on to her stomach and backside.

"I would have called the dry cleaner you told me about," he said, "but I wasn't sure what was arranged and Malvern's out of the way for me. Normally, over here in Jersey would be out of my way, too, but like I said, I have an appointment and you were close by, so I thought I would drop the suit off and let you take care of it."

Wonderful, she thought. She lived an hour from Malvern herself, and now she would have to truck the suit over because it was out of *his* way. She reminded herself that she often told Anthony that one had to correct one's mistakes. She was paying to correct this one, that was for sure. Forcing a smile, she said, "Yes, of course. I'd be happy to."

"Are you sure?" He glanced around the kitchen as if just realizing she wasn't a woman with a lot of free time.

"Yes. It's no problem at all. Thank you for allowing me to do this for you."

She felt like an idiot. What had started out as a way to make amends for a mistake and set a good example for her son seemed ludicrous now, with the man in her house and her having to drive way out of her way just to get a suit cleaned. It was the teacher in her that made her go to extremes in lessons. Maybe she'd start a Teachers Anonymous. There had to be others like her who needed help with their lecture compulsions.

"I'm glad I could help." He frowned, as if he hadn't expected to say that. "I'll go get the suit for you."

"Okay." She followed him to her front door and out to his car. "Are you a Phillies fan?"

He shook his head, chuckling in wry amusement. "Not me. Baseball's about the last sport I like. I was there on business."

Her heart sank on hearing he hated baseball. "I thought so."

He turned around. "You did?"

"You were there in a business suit, usually a sure giveaway. A lot of companies own a block of season tickets and use them for entertainment purposes." She could hear the sarcasm underlying her tone.

"My company doesn't own them," he said quickly. "An advertising company owns them. I was their guest that night."

"Oh." She smiled a little. "What's your business? That is, if I'm not being too nosy."

"No. I own a small chain of pizzerias in Delaware. Cove Pizzerias."

She'd expected almost any other answer than that one. "You? Pizzas?"

He nodded. "What's so strange about that?"

She wasn't willing to say that the last thing he looked like was a pizza man. "I don't know. I don't go to Delaware much, I'm afraid, so I never heard of your chain."

He shrugged, as if not surprised or bruised by her answer. "Like I said, it's a small chain."

His car was a late-model Mercedes, something that didn't surprise her. He looked elegant and expensive, so why shouldn't his car? Still, pizzerias! Her brain was reeling from the incongruity of that one. She wondered if he could actually make a pizza or if he was some kind of corporate wunderkind investor. Probably he didn't know his mozzarella from his yeast cake.

"Do you really make pizzas?" she blurted out.

He had the car door open and the suit in his hands. "Of course. I said so . . . didn't I?"

"No." She shook her head. "I mean, do you actually make them yourself?"

He laughed. Something about the way his lips curved upward, as if he were surprised and pleased, tugged at her heart.

"I have in the past, but not anymore," he said. "I made them eighteen hours a day when I was first getting started."

"Oh."

"I still make a mean pizza."

The genuine smile lighting up his face gave him an innocent look. He lost all that overlay of sophistication and experience and became, for one instant, like her son, hovering between childhood and adulthood.

Not her son, she acknowledged, as another swell of warmth poured through her. Her lips were suddenly dry, and her breasts ached. The feelings he invoked in her were hardly motherly.

She forced away the sensations and smiled back. "That I'd like to see."

The moment the words came out of her mouth, she realized how much they sounded as if she were fishing for an invitation—or even trying to get something romantic started. Before she could scramble up a disclaimer, he chuckled and said, "I guess I don't look much like I can do it now, do I?"

She nodded, relief washing through her. "Not much."

"What do you do?" he asked.

"I teach seventh-grade social studies." She made a face. "There's nothing worse than adolescents in the first throes of puberty—especially as I have one of mine own now too. It's like being in a war zone sometimes. The only saving grace for Anthony is that I teach in a different school district than he is in. He'd die of embarrassment if Mom were his teacher."

"You don't look like you're tough enough to handle a class of crazed teenagers."

She touched her falling-down hair and shrugged. "Sometimes I don't think I am either."

"Were you . . . were you really with those women that night?"

She laughed at his hesitation. "Yes. We've all had season tickets in that row for years and became friends over time. We call ourselves the Widows' Club now, for obvious reasons. They're a little crazy, but it's good to see older people really enjoying life the way they do."

He grinned back. "I liked them. You should have heard them going on about you getting french fries." He started laughing. "And you coming into the men's room like that . . . You're just as crazy as they are, Elaine."

She liked the way he said her name.

The more she looked at him, the more she knew he definitely had the solid build that comes with maturity—not fat, but not that slight, almost vulnerable torso that men have in their early twenties. His features also had a maturity that comes from experience . . . sexual experience . . . that wonderful knowing look that went right to a woman's sensuality. In an instant a woman could feel attractive and, more important, attracting. Those sorts of feelings tended to go out of a woman's life with marriage and children.

Elaine pushed away the notion. She was reacting like a teenager rather than a woman. Maybe there was something to be said for having sex just for the sake of sex. Maybe if she had practiced that at some point after Joe died, she wouldn't be having a case of raging hormones the first time she was truly attracted to a man—like now. Granted, she'd never been attracted like this, but she would probably be coping with it better.

Another problem occurred to her. She'd been standing out here with a man in front of all her neighbors. They might be in their houses, but she had no doubt Graham Reed had been duly noted for future gossip swaps. She felt embarrassed and yet couldn't help feeling a little proud too. Even if this was an innocent encounter, it did look as if she weren't sexually dead. Nothing grated on a woman's ego more than to be seen as "on the shelf," whether she privately preferred to be there or not.

She shivered, rubbing her arms against the chill air.

"We better go in," he said, and ushered her back into the house.

The moment they entered the kitchen, they found water spewing out of the top of the washer. It ran like a lovely bubbling cascade down the lemon yellow front panel and along the floor until it was stopped by the piles of clothing waiting their turn. A turn that would never happen now. The dryer still chugged happily, ignoring the failings of its mate.

"Oh, no!" Elaine wailed, diving for the floor in a futile attempt to stop the water with the dirty clothes before it did damage to anything else.

A pair of long male legs stepped over her and her dirty laundry. She watched as expensive leather loafers walked straight through the flowing water to the washer, where Graham very sensibly turned off the machine. He turned off the dryer, too, as a precaution, while Elaine pushed the clothes along the floor in a mop-up operation. She cursed heartily in a chain of foul words that never once repeated themselves. Every time she got near this guy, she acted like an idiot.

"You've been hanging around men's rooms for a long time, haven't you?" he asked, amused.

"No, just Cleo and Jean," she muttered, glancing up at him, thoroughly embarrassed. "I can't believe this! My washer!"

He took off his suit jacket. "I bet it's got something stuck in the drain trap. Sometimes things don't shred down small enough like they're supposed to and get caught, especially in older machines like this one. Has it ever happened before?"

She sat back on her heels, amazed. "Yes, once. And the repairman said something about the washer drain being clogged. How do you know all this?"

"Because I used to have a washer that did that, way back in my lean years. After about ten loads, it would pick up enough lint and jam the drain. It was having to be fixed all the time, so I learned to fix it myself." He began to roll up his sleeves. "Got a screwdriver? I'll take off the back and clean it out."

"Oh, no, I couldn't let you do that," she said,

even as a part of her brain berated her for letting a free fix-it get away. It just wouldn't be right to have him do it, though.

"You're cleaning my suit," he countered reasonably.

Tempting, but her conscience said, "You have an appointment."

"I'll call." He stepped back over her to the telephone, lifted the receiver, and began dialing.

"If you fix my washer in that suit, do I have to get it clean too?" she asked in a last-ditch effort to divert him.

He laughed. "This one's on me. . . . Jerry? I'm delayed . . ."

Elaine knelt on the floor, wiping fruitlessly as the flood spread wider and wider. Out of the corner of her eye she watched Graham speak into the phone. Not only did he set off all kinds of sensual longings within her, but he wanted to fix her washer. Gratis. God, what a hero!

A subdued "poof" sounded behind her. At the same moment, she felt a flash of heat and caught a whiff of burning. She turned. Her eyes widened in horror at the sight of her forgotten cooking now a fire burning merrily on her stovetop. Dark smoke billowed out and flames were already licking at the overhead wooden cabinets.

"*Fire!*" she screamed, trying to scramble upright to put it out. Her feet slipped out from under her on the wet floor, delaying her from reaching the latest catastrophe.

"Where's your fire extinguisher?" Graham shouted, somehow already at the stove.

"Oh, God!" she wailed, trying to remember in which cabinet she'd stored it. She started ripping open cabinet doors to try to find the damn thing.

"Okay, it's out," Graham said calmly.

She whipped around to find him standing at the sink, setting the pan, the *covered* pan, in it. He turned the water on to cool the metal and put out the last flames still running along the outside of the pan. No fire was on the stove any longer, either. He'd simply stuck the lid on the pan and effectively smothered the flames, then removed it and turned off the gas burner, killing that fire too.

Her face grew hot with shame at how stupid she must look to him. Somehow, "gauche" became the living word whenever he was around.

"It looks like it was just grease burning off," he went on, lifting the copper-bottomed pan for her to see through the smoky haze in the room. "There's just soot on the pan now. That ought to wash away. What were you cooking?"

"Sausage, then green peppers and onions for spaghetti sauce," she whispered, wanting only to die.

"Homemade sauce. Well, you need to be careful about leaving food to fry by itself," he warned sensibly.

She nodded. On the wall above him was the plaque that read, The Best Person for the Job Is a Woman. It had been given to her as a joke when she'd applied for an assistant principal's job and had lost it to a man. But the plaque was all wrong, and she had just proved it. Graham must think she was a full-blooded, raving lunatic. He would be right.

"I'll go open the windows to let the smoke out," he said.

As he left the kitchen on his next mercy mission, she knew he'd find every other room in the house just as much of a disaster as this one.

Her humiliation complete, she carefully closed her cabinet doors and lay face down on the floor, not caring that it was wet, not caring that she looked ridiculous. She felt overwhelmed, incompetent, and inadequate, and lying on the floor beat the hell out of crying.

Water began to penetrate her clothes almost immediately. A hair shirt couldn't be as effective a punishment, she thought, hearing footsteps returning. They paused at the entryway. She knew she ought to get up, but decided not to bother. Might as well give him further evidence that she was a nut case.

"What are you doing?" he asked.

"Lying down to die," she replied. "I know when I'm licked. Just leave me for the buzzards. They'll be along eventually."

He laughed, coming over to her. "You fit in that Widows' Club of yours very well."

She didn't lift her head. "Yes, that's right. I'm Dumbo."

"Here." He took her by the hands and hauled her upright.

"You could have put your back out," she said by way of thanks.

"It would be worth it."

She realized he was staring at her breasts, their shape visible with nipples puckered, under her now wet sweatshirt. The heat flooding her body changed from humiliation to desire in a second. Her breath caught in her throat, leaving her without words to protest against that fierce desire.

His gaze rose, focusing on her mouth. Her lips felt dry, so dry. She ran her tongue around them. He groaned and bent his head toward hers. . . . She felt her eyelids flutter closed. . . .

It was a gentle kiss, soft and tentative, their lips brushing together for one timeless moment.

Graham raised his head and stepped back. Elaine opened her eyes, feeling as if she'd been spun off a dizzying height.

He cleared his throat, looking away as if he were embarrassed this time. "I better get to work on this washer, so you can get your laundry done."

She found her voice, although it was shaky. "There are tools in the pantry. That door there, past the dryer. Bottom shelf."

She knelt down and began mopping up her floor again as he found the tools and unloaded her underwear load. He didn't seem to care about his shirt and suit trousers, although he didn't get a drop of water on either as far as she could tell.

Despite all that had happened, a tiny smile played at the corner of her mouth. She had been kissed.

She could almost hear Cleo saying, "Oh, honey, what a man!"

Graham torqued the last screw on the back panel snug, then said, "That's it. Should be good as new."

"Thanks," Elaine said as she tried to wedge herself between the pulled-out washer and the dryer to see. Graham didn't move, for it brought her dangerously close to him before she straightened.

Her lips had tasted so sweet, he thought. And innocent. He didn't know how that had been managed by a mature woman with a child, but it had. He wanted to taste her kiss again, just to see if it felt the same a second time.

"I can't believe it was tissues that caused the problem," she said, her voice filled with disgust. She slipped away to finish the last of her floor mopping before he gave in to the urge to reach for her again. "I was positive I emptied the pockets of my bathrobe before I did that first load."

Bathrobe meant bathing. He remembered the old *Dick Van Dyke Show* episode when Laura had stuck her toe in the tub faucet and then couldn't get it out. Elaine would do something like that. He'd love to play Mr. Fix-It with her stuck in the tub . . . naked . . . soapy water lapping at her breasts . . .

He better stop this, he thought, straightening from his task. He squeezed out from behind the washer, saying, "Let's turn it on and let it drain, to see if it's working right before I push it back."

She nodded, and as she walked back to the washer, she seemed to avoid getting too close to him. He wondered if she was as confused as he was about that unexpected kiss. He liked the thought. And this was nice, too, helping her out. Saving her would probably be more accurate, he admitted in amusement. But he had felt good and, more important, needed by someone in a very basic way. And she made him laugh. When he had come in to find her lying on the floor, waiting for the buzzards, he had been tickled. He couldn't think of a better word than just plain *tickled* about her. He liked the way she handled her problems with humor. He had thought the three older women had been crazy, but Elaine was the nuttiest of them all.

Yet when he'd lifted her to her feet and seen her breasts perfectly outlined under her wet sweatshirt, something far more potent than amusement had rushed through him.

"Looks good," he pronounced as the drain sucked down the wash water with a loud, quick slurp. He shut the washer off and pushed it back against the wall with Elaine helping. She was a distraction, but he was careful not to let his trousers or shirt touch anything. So far he'd been successful in keeping himself from getting spots, though his shoes were probably ruined from the water on the floor. He wasn't telling Elaine, though. She'd probably want to fly him to London for a new bench-made pair.

"I don't know how to thank you," she said when they finished. "You've been wonderful."

"I didn't mind." Those good feelings about being needed were surfacing again. "I don't know how you manage alone."

"A lot of prayer and the number of a reliable repairman," she replied, grinning wryly.

He laughed, then sobered. "How long has it been since your husband passed away?"

"Nearly two years."

A long silence ensued. Elaine gazed at him, then looked away as if nervous and unsure of herself. He had no idea why she should be nervous or unsure around him.

"Who won the other night?" he asked finally, breaking the silence.

"I thought you weren't a fan."

He shrugged. "I'm not really. Just curious."

"Phillies."

"I'm surprised you're not at a game tonight."

"The team's on a road trip." She glanced at her watch. "In fact, the game should be on the TV now."

The conversation dwindled again.

"I better go," he said, putting on his suit jacket. He went over to the table, where he'd dropped the stained suit when they'd caught sight of the flood, and handed it to her.

"Thanks," she said. Her fingers didn't touch his as she took it from him. Instead they unconsciously smoothed down the suit lapels as she held it over her arm. The physical heat started flowing again inside him as he watched.

He cleared his throat and headed for the front door. She followed him out like the last time, still carrying the suit.

When they reached his car, she said, "If you'll give me your number, I'll call you when it's done."

"I'll check in with you next week," he said, knowing he'd be in and out of his office for the next several days and might miss her call. Besides, if he called her, he could ensure it was a good time to talk on his end; whereas if she called him and caught him at a bad time when he could only take the information and nothing more, he'd never have the excuse to call her back.

She had a funny look on her face, as if she'd swallowed a dose of something less than palatable, but all she said was, "I'll ask Nancy to have it ready by next Monday so you can pick it up any time after that."

He nodded and got into the car. After starting it, he waved and rolled down his window, saying, "I'll call you next week."

She smiled. "No problem. Bye now."

"Bye."

She didn't wait and watch as he drove off, but

went straight back into her house. He wondered what she thought of him and hoped it was good. He wasn't sure why her opinion mattered so much, but it did.

As he turned the corner of her complex, next week seemed a long way away, like his next birthday when he'd been a kid or waiting for Christmas or summer vacation from school.

Still, he knew the wait would be well worth it.

"So much for that," Elaine muttered, slamming the front door shut behind her.

Okay, so he was an attractive man. He had been wonderful in two crises that would have had just about anyone else running around like a headless chicken—she'd certainly done her fair imitation of one. He'd kissed her, too, and it had been almost like a wonderful first kiss ever, all over again. Despite the calamities, she'd been flying.

But then he'd refused to give her his phone number, acting as though she were about to throw herself at him at any moment. He couldn't have made himself clearer. The kiss was a mistake, and he was uninterested in her. Maybe he even thought her beneath his "station," him being rich now and she being a poor idiot. One would have thought that stuff had gone out with the French Revolution, but now she wondered.

At least she'd handled herself well, she thought, dumping his expensive suit on one of the kitchen chairs. The other members of the Widows' Club, who took no garbage from anyone, would have been proud of her poise. If and when she was ready to date again, she'd choose the person very carefully. Not some sophisticated snob who didn't even like baseball. Didn't even like it!

Or maybe he was just a nice man who had kissed her out of pity. That thought was even worse than the others.

Still, he was really sexy. . . .

"Look at you," she muttered. She was swinging from one side of the emotional pendulum to the other. She didn't need that. Nope, not one bit.

She'd get his damn suit cleaned and get it out of her house just as fast as she could. Her kitchen was a disaster with still more cleaning up to do, as well as sauce half made and waiting to be finished, but she didn't mind at all.

She flipped on the radio, rolling the dial channel to the station that carried the Phillies games. She'd have to skip the televised version, what with the night ahead of her. Immediately the radio blared the current tug-of-war strategies of pitcher against batter.

Life was good, life was normal in all its chaos, and men in Armani suits could cool their heels at her door from now on.

THREE

As Graham shouldered his way through the crowds climbing up the wide concrete ramp of Veterans Stadium, he asked himself what he was doing here again. He didn't like baseball, he wanted no part of Ed's advertising schemes for Cove Pizzerias, and he was swamped with work with the busy summer season coming up.

It must be the french fries, he decided, as the wonderful smell of cooked potatoes and salt wafted through the air. All that cholesterol was too much to resist. And the Vet had the best. He knew. He had it on good authority.

The good authority was why he was really there.

"I want to get some fries," he told Ed, who looked at him as if he'd grown two heads. He could feel his face actually flushing and hoped Ed didn't notice in the stadium lights.

"Sure," Ed replied, clearly willing to go along with anything if it got Cove Pizzerias into his company's advertising fold.

It wouldn't be the first time he'd made an idiot of himself, Graham thought, as he considered why he was at the game. Look at the way he'd gone unannounced to Elaine's house, taking advantage of her address on her card to drop off the suit, a poor excuse at best. Meeting or no meeting in Cherry Hill on the possibilities of expanding into New Jersey, he hadn't had to stop by her place. But he had. The only redeeming grace was that her house had practically fallen down around them, and he'd been able to fix the problems. It gave him a funny feeling to remember how good he had felt when he'd walked out of her house that night.

She was like forbidden fruit to him, a widow with a child. Home and hearth were more important to her than any corporate deals. That lured him in subtle, deeply physical ways.

He wanted to see if those good feelings came back without cleaned suits, stove fires, and jammed washers in the way of things. He wanted to see if that kiss, so sweet and so innocent and so packed with the promise of sensuality, held up days afterward.

Graham got the fries and a beer for good measure at a concession stand, allowing Ed to pay after the man insisted.

"I hope those women aren't here again," Ed

said as they made their way around the 300 section to their seats.

Graham shot him a look of disapproval. "They were enjoying the game."

"Yes, of course." Ed smoothed over his faux pas quickly, changing the subject. "We went into intensive on your ad campaign and came up with the brainstorm of a collage of rapid-fire, evoking images with a voice saying 'Cove Pizzerias' at the end. That's it through the whole thing, just 'Cove Pizzerias.' Very de trop, *very* artistic. These would be short, ten-second ads, strategically placed on key TV markets—"

"That's just too expensive for Cove," Graham said. Ed obviously had a vision of turning Cove Pizzerias into the next Domino's in one season. Well, the man had signaled that he was still all business by wearing his suit to the game. Graham had chosen to dress more casually, dumped sodas notwithstanding.

"Okay." Ed launched into another set of "intensives" as they found their seats.

Graham settled into his with a sigh of disappointment. The other seats around them were empty, and he realized they must belong to Ed's company. But more important, the seats directly behind him were empty. Maybe she wasn't coming.

His stomach turned sour at the thought.

The stands filled as the start of the game got closer. The seats behind him stayed empty until less than five minutes was left. Graham was wondering if he could fake an illness and leave now that his personal mission was scrubbed, when Elaine's son appeared out of the concourse entrance below. Graham watched the boy turn right and walk purposefully up the concrete steps, followed by the three older women. Older, he thought, but certainly not elderly. Every one looked vivacious in her own way. They chattered back and forth, their conversation clearly interesting because the boy was grinning. All of them carried game paraphernalia from seat cushions to small coolers.

Graham eyed Anthony and considered that he looked like an easygoing child rather than a brat. But the boy's demeanor didn't change Graham's outlook about other people's children. They meant a commitment of some sort on his part if he dated the mother. He barely had time for a relationship with a woman, so how could he put in the extra effort involved with a child? He couldn't. He knew it and knew it wasn't fair even to contemplate such a thing.

Elaine emerged from the entrance, and all his good intentions disappeared in a wave of sensual desire. She glanced up into the stands, directly at him. If he had called out to her and she heard him, her stance couldn't have been more telling. She stilled for an endless moment, gazing up at him from under that red Phillies cap she wore. He wanted to take her in his arms and kiss her senseless, feel her body pressed to his. Signals seemed to cross the distance between them, signals he couldn't put into words but understood with his body. She moved finally, following her personal crowd up the steps to their seats.

Graham felt released from a spell as their gazes broke. The test results were eye-opening. If anything, his reaction to her was stronger than ever. Guilt assailed him as he wondered if she was still grieving for her husband, even after two years. She hadn't seemed to be, but then he hadn't thought much beyond his attraction to her.

He noticed the bundle she carried of a small seat cushion, a quilt, a loaded backpack, and a baseball mitt. Clearly she was a veteran of ball games, especially those on cool spring evenings. He could feel the chill already infiltrating his lightweight wool slacks and leather bomber jacket. But all the things she carried indicated a joie de vivre, not mourning black and tears. If she still grieved, it didn't show. Things might be safer for him if it did.

Conversation caught his ears as the women drew closer and filed into their row behind him.

". . . I did *not* deliberately set out to be late, Mary! How many times do I have to tell you that?"

"Jean, you are always late. You were even late for Bob's funeral."

"I was not! The limo driver missed the turn."

"For nearly an hour?"

Cleo's voice chimed in. "Jean, honey, you'd still be late even if your house was burning down. And you *were* late for your man's funeral. Saint Peter will be waiting at the pearly gates for you, saying,

'Lord have mercy, child, but you were supposed to be here ten years ago.' "

The three older women burst out laughing as they settled into their seats. Graham couldn't help a small smile of amusement at the conversation. They had that joie de vivre too.

He continued to watch Elaine out of the corner of his eye. He understood exactly why she was friends with these women. Long ago he had had friends like that, who teased good-naturedly and would give the shirts off their backs if it was needed. Now he realized he couldn't name one true friend he still had.

Next to him Ed groaned. Graham's smile vanished.

"Watch your soda today, Elaine," one of the women said as Elaine disappeared from his view. He could sense her coming into the row and sitting down. "Mr. Suit is here again."

Graham turned and smiled briefly at Elaine. "Hi."

"Hi." She smiled a tiny smile back, as if shy. Her reaction made him feel like a schoolboy again.

Her son glared at him. Graham felt the dislike hit him with a slap. Somehow that hurt even as it sobered him to his foolish behavior.

"You boys gonna cheer this time?" Cleo asked, tapping him and Ed on the shoulder. She didn't wait for an answer. "I expect to hear some cheering now."

"Cleo."

It was Elaine's voice. Just the name said in a no-nonsense manner, but even Graham could feel the underlying whip-crack to it. He reassessed his first thoughts about how Elaine dealt with adolescent students. She was probably good at it.

"I'm just telling them to be enthusiastic, Ms. Schoolteacher," Cleo said. "Nothing wrong in that, giving these boys a little buck-up now."

"A little buck-up is what you're causing," the woman named Jean muttered. "In fact, substitute that 'b' with an—"

Beads clacked loudly and furiously, stifling any further conversation.

Ed leaned over and whispered, "I'll go get an usher to stop this."

"No." Graham could hear the heavy forceful-ness in his voice. He toned it down. "No. They're not bothering me."

Ed gaped at him. "Not bothering you! She whacked you on the shoulder and told you to cheer, for God's sake!"

"Let them alone," was all Graham said.

He was making a fool of himself enough already, he thought, without a full-fledged spectacle of ushers throwing four women and a boy out of the stadium. But he couldn't stop himself and couldn't explain why. This woman, widow and mother, had a lure that he couldn't ignore. If he could leave gracefully, he would, but he'd boxed himself in. Maybe the dumped soda had frozen his brains, and he hadn't yet recovered.

"Tommy Greene's pitching tonight," Elaine said to her group after the national anthem was played. "His ERA to start the season is almost a 4. But if he throws some K's tonight, he'll bring that down some, right, Anthony?"

Graham had no idea what she was talking about, but he had to admit he was impressed by the way she talked it. He wouldn't have thought a woman would be so interested in a male-dominated sport. From the female murmurs of agreement behind him, clearly the others knew what she was talking about.

Her son said, "Don't worry about Tommy, Mom. He's a hard worker. His ERA'll be in the low 3's before the season's halfway over."

From the admiring tone in the kid's voice, Graham realized this was an important player for him. He sat, pondering and listening, and becoming even more interested—and confused—as the game went on for several innings. Mindful of Cleo behind him, he actually clapped when something good happened to the home team. Ed sat and glowered. Graham decided it was worth coming just to see the man stew.

But the one thing he was aware of all the time was Elaine behind him. Right behind him. Every movement, every shift of her body, sent a shudder of awareness through his until he felt as if he would burst from holding himself back.

He couldn't take any more when he felt her stand up and move away from her place. He turned to see her coming out onto the steps and walking down. With all the ball game survival things she'd brought, he had a pretty good idea where she was headed.

He had the urge to get up and follow her down and accost her in the concourse, away from the prying eyes of Ed and her companions and son. But that would be so obvious. And he'd already gone over all the reasons why any interest in her was a mistake. So to go down and waylay her would be a worse mistake.

Still, he was owed a payback for the men's room incident.

He got up and stretched, saying, "I'm going to the men's room."

Ed let him by without a blink. The peanut gallery behind him were as silent as statues. Anthony was too young to recognize what he was doing, though he had a feeling he didn't fool the three women much.

He wondered what Elaine's reaction would be.

Elaine dried her hands as the ladies' room traffic poured around her. She glanced into the last mirror near the exit door and let out her breath, suddenly aware she was holding it. Sitting behind Graham was more of a torture than she'd expected. Unfortunately, she hadn't expected anything that night and had almost passed out when she'd caught sight of him in the stands. She'd had to use the excuse of the bathroom just to give herself some breathing space.

Not too bad, she thought, examining her appearance. For an idiot middle-aged lady. Nearly middle-aged lady, she corrected herself. She hadn't gotten there quite yet. Still, she wished she were that famous ten and ten—ten years younger and ten pounds lighter. Maybe a little lipstick would help, she mused, although she knew nothing truly would. She was what she was. She got the small tube out anyway and began to carefully apply the dark red color to her upper lip.

"How's my suit?"

At the sound of the male voice, Elaine yelped, along with the rest of the women in the ladies' room. Her hand jerked and a streak of lipstick stretched across her lower cheek. She caught herself but it was too late. In the mirror it looked as if she'd flunked out of clown school. At least she knew who it was . . . and he wasn't actually in the room. He was just outside the exit door, calling over the concrete block modesty wall.

"You scared me!" she accused, grabbing up some paper towels and wetting and soaping them in order to correct the damage. She rubbed at the streak. "And you scared all the rest of the women in here."

"That's nothing compared to what you did in the men's room last time," he said loudly.

Women gave her dirty looks. Elaine scrubbed her face harder. The lipstick seemed to be made out of superglue. Even though it was off, it still left a faint mark on her face.

"I'll be right out!" she called, determined to get the lipstick off totally and to silence any further conversation.

"Take your time. So how's my suit? I didn't have a chance to call you yet—"

"Graham!" She found herself grinning into the mirror, despite her acute embarrassment. Clearly he had a sense of whimsy, and she couldn't help liking him for it. But talk about tables being turned . . .

"Can't this wait?" a woman asked her crossly.

"I'm trying, lady," she muttered, scrubbing harder.

"What? I can't hear you."

"Go away!"

"I'll wait."

"I talked to him once in the men's room," she said to no one in general, "and now he's getting me back."

Several women actually laughed. She didn't feel quite so bad. The lipstick was cleaned off, but half her face was red from the scrubbing. She decided she'd live with it, so she dumped the towels in the wastebasket and hurried out of the ladies' room. Graham was right outside.

"What was that? Payback time?" she asked.

"Maybe. What happened to your face?"

She automatically put her hand to her cheek.

"Let's just say that lipstick never belongs anywhere but *on* the lips."

He grinned. "Did I catch you at a bad time?"

"Just mutilating myself. And your suit is fine. In fact, I'm supposed to pick it up tomorrow."

"Good. I'll be over the day after to get it. Okay?"

"Okay."

Despite her flush of embarrassment that he *had* noticed her cheek, she couldn't help wishing she had taken the time to actually get lipstick on her lips.

It didn't matter, though, when she found him staring at her mouth. Those same strong sensations she had felt that night at her house surged along her veins. She wanted him to kiss her again.

A woman squeezed around them, breaking the spell. Graham blinked, then backed up a step. Without a word he took Elaine's arm, guiding her out of the line of traffic. He began to stroll down the concourse.

"Where are we going?" she asked as they passed by their stadium entrance. She was aware of his hand at her elbow . . . and his body brushing against hers as they walked.

"Just taking a walk around the concourse. I don't know about you, but I need a break from our audience. Besides, I just wanted to talk to you."

"Oh." She wondered how they'd explain their absence, then decided she'd cross that bridge when they came to it. The lure of a man's regard was too much to worry about questions afterward.

"How's the washer?" He chuckled. "And the stove?"

"They're both fine." She shook her head. "I'm normally not like that."

"What are you like, then?"

The question seemed suggestive. She wanted it to be and wanted to answer it in kind. She pushed away the notion. "I . . . I don't know. Normal. Not an idiot, certainly."

He laughed. "Don't ruin the image."

"Thanks a bunch," she muttered.

She wondered why he was at the game, a question that had nagged at her ever since she'd spotted him in the stands. He said he didn't care for baseball. A wayward thought occurred that maybe he had come just to see her. That, she knew, was completely ridiculous. He was with the other man, so it was business again. It had to be. What was wrong with her that she couldn't control her reaction to him?

"Do you want a soda for cover this time?" he asked. Then he grinned, tapping his leather jacket. "I dressed prepared for the shower."

She chuckled. "I've sworn off soda from now on."

A roar went up inside the stadium. Elaine glanced up at one of the TV screens hanging from brackets on the wall, installed to ensure no one could miss the action while at the concession stands. A player was rounding the bases.

She groaned. "Darren Daulton just hit a home run, and I missed it!"

"I guess this is my version of spilling soda," Graham said. "If I hadn't started this walk, you would have been back in your seat."

"It's okay." Inside she was cursing her luck, but she had to admit his attention was flattering enough to give up at least one home run. "You take your chances when you go to the bathroom. Lord knows what else I missed."

"Nothing much, I don't think," he said, smiling. "Someone got on base, I think. Maybe a triple. I'm not sure."

"Hell," she muttered. "That was probably Kruk or Hollins. I left right after the second batter struck out. Mariano doesn't know the meaning of a walk."

Graham looked puzzled. "What do you mean?"

"Mariano Duncan," she said. "He likes to swing the bat. It's got to be over his head or behind him before he doesn't swing at it. That's his strength and his weakness. But he's working on it."

"Oh."

That "Oh" said more than a "How boring" could ever express, she admitted ruefully, feeling oddly hurt by his lack of interest. Why she should be hurt, she couldn't fathom. He had said right from the beginning he wasn't a fan of the game.

It only proved how far her daydreams had wandered. Things were getting out of hand inside her in more than one way. Heat crept up into her cheeks as she realized how she'd gone on and on about something he didn't like. Maybe she was venturing into male territory further than she'd thought.

"How's your business going with that advertising man?" she asked. She was trying to be polite and get her mind back up to gutter level, then she wondered if she'd made a social mistake. His business was none of her business.

He shrugged. "I don't know. He has grandiose ideas, a little too rich for a time when the economy is making a steady comeback but not a spectacular one. Whenever you do advertising, you take a hit up front financially but with the calculated risk that it will repay itself several times over in more business. But the kind of media blitz Ed's proposing is just not cost-effective for Cove Pizzerias."

"One of the teachers at school has had your pizzas," Elaine volunteered. "She said they were super. Maybe you want to consider expanding your customer base. A lot of people travel through Delaware. Or shop there because of the lack of a sales tax."

She realized that by telling him about a teacher's opinion, she was revealing that she'd talked about him. It smacked of teenage girls discussing boys while in the school lavatory. Another bad sign of the state of her libido.

"Maybe," he said, "but I don't think it's enough to merit a radio/TV promotion expense."

Elaine knew her face was now as red as her cap. She could feel the hot flush bathing her cheeks and throat. Of course he would dismiss her advice. What did a social studies teacher know about advertising? Nothing.

Except that she was a consumer who knew where she heard things and paid attention to product-toting.

"I'm sure you're right," she said.

"Well, you could be," he conceded, politely generous.

"I doubt it. My forte is teaching."

"Your forte is more than teaching."

He pulled her over, away from the crowds on the concourse and into a cubbyhole of darkness. Before she could ask what he was doing, his mouth came down on hers.

The kiss in no way resembled the sweet one of the other night. This one was fire and passion, demand and need. She clutched his shoulders to steady herself, her fingers digging into his jacket. His arms held her tightly against him. She could feel every inch of his body pressed to hers. But his mouth . . . his mouth fit perfectly, his tongue searching hers out until they swirled together with the sensual promise of more intimate interaction between man and woman. Yearning, long dormant, rocked her with its intensity. She wanted to rock her hips against his as need pooled deep inside her, but somehow she held back the wanton movement.

Finally he raised his head. His eyes were glazed with desire. "You are truly something."

"Really?" She became aware of people passing not far from them, staring into their shelter, which now seemed as open as the pitcher's mound in a World Series game. Guilt dragged at her, guilt for a husband who had been a good man and a good father. Maybe she wasn't as ready for this as she thought.

Graham must have sensed something of her feelings, for he loosened his embrace. "Somehow I don't think either one of us wants to explain this one."

She stepped away, reluctantly and yet relieved. "I don't think so either."

They emerged back onto the concourse. Elaine figured they had walked halfway around to the outfield entrances. They'd have to backtrack to reach their seats. At least he didn't have telltale lipstick on his mouth.

"Well, I'll let you get back to the game," he said awkwardly. "I'll go get a souvenir or something."

She nodded and waved good-bye, hurrying around to their section. When she reached it, she headed out into the large bowl. The sound and fury of fans in a pandemonium slapped her in the face and lifted her heart at the same time. Not even the Phils getting their last out of the inning could deter the feeling. She had it bad this year, she admitted. And if she wasn't careful, she'd have something else bad too.

If she didn't already.

Graham was all wrong for her. She should walk away now and keep on going. That was the smart thing to do.

Inside her somewhere was a little voice that made a raspberry noise at the smart thing to do.

When she took her seat again, the three widows were on her instantly.

"You see your suit?" Cleo asked in a whisper that could be heard in Atlantic City.

"He's not my suit," Elaine said, smiling at Anthony, who was staring wide-eyed at her, unsure. She pulled his cap down on his forehead in a rough-and-tumble gesture of affection, then said to her cohorts, "I went to the bathroom, remember?"

"You could have run into him on the concourse," Jean said.

Elaine didn't answer. She didn't dare.

"Silence is golden," Mary said, smiling like an angel. "And telling."

The advertising man in front of her caused her the most anxiety. He turned around and gave her such a menacing glare, she wondered how anyone could look so offended when she hadn't done anything. Except that she had. She'd kissed Graham. And she wanted him badly.

The object of her thoughts came out of the concourse entrance. He was empty-handed, his search for a souvenir gone unrewarded. He turned up the stairway and turned those magnificent brown eyes directly on her. His gaze held hers relentlessly, just as it had each time before. Her heart beat harder and faster against her breastbone.

"My, my," Cleo murmured. "He's fine looking."

"Cleo," Elaine said in a low voice, while trying to regain her emotional equilibrium. She glanced at Anthony, trying to signal to Cleo that she was giving the boy unnecessary ideas. The three had been teasing her long before Graham, but this was too close.

"I'm just saying," Cleo protested. "Look at Jimmy catch that ball, Anthony."

Outfielder Jim Eisenriech specialized in shagging fly balls, let alone pop-ups as tame as the one he'd just caught. It didn't fool Anthony. He said, "Even I could have caught that one."

"You're getting too smart for your age, boy," Cleo muttered. To Elaine's horror, the woman turned her attention to Graham as he made his way past the other people in his row. Cleo didn't say anything, just stared at him. The other two caught on and followed her lead. A scientist dissecting an insect under a microscope couldn't have done a more thorough job.

"God help me," Elaine murmured, feeling as if she were with the female version of the Three Stooges. She wouldn't have been surprised if they started doing pratfalls. It'd be less embarrassing.

"Is something wrong, ladies?" Graham asked, having caught sight of the staring contest as he turned to sit down.

"I'm out of here," Elaine muttered to herself, vowing never to go to the bathroom again.

"Nothing's wrong," Cleo said loudly. "Just wondering why you're empty-handed, that's all."

"Was I supposed to bring back something for you?" he asked, grinning.

"I would have liked a soda," Mary said. Elaine turned to her in surprise. Usually Mary was the last to begin the mischief, not the first.

"A hot dog would have been good for me," Jean added.

"This is ridiculous!" the other man exploded. "I'm finding an usher to stop this harassment."

"Omigod!" Elaine moaned, scrunching down and trying to wedge herself under the plastic seat.

"Don't be ridiculous, Ed," Graham said. "Sit down." Ed sat. "The ladies aren't hurting either of us. Are you?"

"If I were a few years younger," Cleo said, "you'd be hurtin' real good."

"Cleo!" Elaine exclaimed. "If you don't stop, *I'll* report you!"

"Mom!" It was Anthony's turn to be horrified.

"It wasn't me," Cleo said. "I only asked him a question. Jean and Mary started giving dinner orders."

The other two just laughed.

"I'm sorry," Elaine said to Graham as she realized she couldn't wedge herself into oblivion. "Sometimes they get out of hand. Worse than children."

She glared at the three women to make her point.

"It's senility," Jean said, unrepentant.

"Hits the stomach first," Mary added. "You want a soda?"

"Sure."

Jean and Mary got up, adroitly escaping the fray. Cleo stuck her foot out, but the two managed to step over it without tripping.

Once they were gone, the others settled back in their seats. Elaine collapsed into hers. She felt as if she'd been caught hanging out on the street corner with the school's most popular boy and had come through it barely scathed. She stared at Graham's back, wondering what he thought of it all. Did he really find her that attractive?

Now, that was ridiculous, she thought. Truly ridiculous.

FOUR

"There's been a little problem."

Elaine's stomach clenched as Nancy disappeared into the back of her dry-cleaning place. Problem, she thought in growing panic. What problem?

"Didn't the stain come out?" she called to her friend.

"It's out."

Nancy came back with Graham's suit in hand. It didn't have a plastic bag over it, a bad dry-cleaning sign, Elaine was sure. But as Nancy emerged fully into the light, the problem became obvious.

"It's purple!" Elaine exclaimed in horror. Graham's gray suit was a lovely shade of lavender. "I only wanted it cleaned, not dyed!"

"I'm sorry, Elaine. Sometimes this happens with silk," Nancy said, hanging the suit on the stand next to the register. She pulled the jacket bottom up, giving Elaine a closer look at the damage. "There's no way to predict that it will happen. You can clean a silk suit a thousand times and it will never turn. You can clean it once and bam! It loses its proper color."

"Oooohhhhh," Elaine moaned, tears pushing at her eyes. She gulped them back. "How am I supposed to explain this to him? I fussed and now I've ruined his suit. He'll kill me!"

She would look like an idiot on top of already looking like an idiot. It was as if the syndrome multiplied upon itself tenfold. The first man she'd been attracted to in ages, and he seemed attracted to her, but how could he like her now? How could she ever face him again? She couldn't. She couldn't.

"My insurance will pay for ten times the cost of the cleaning," Nancy said helpfully. "I'm really sorry, Elaine."

"I know." Insurance. She liked the sound of that. "How much would that be?"

"About two hundred." Nancy sighed. "I tell you what, I'll add a hundred to it. That should help."

Hope rose in her heart. Repayment would help. "Okay. I'll take it."

Her friend smiled, guilt clearing away quickly. "I'll put in a claim tomorrow. You ought to have the check in about three weeks."

"But I'm supposed to give him the suit tonight!"

"It's the best I can do."

The walls closed in on her for one long, terrible moment, like a trap.

"Get him another one and substitute it," Nancy said.

Elaine pushed the darkness away in a burst of hope. It immediately deflated. "It's an Armani. I have no idea where to get one, let alone get exactly the same one."

"Go to Boyd's in Center City," Nancy said with a wave of dismissal. "They carry every suit and designer brand imaginable. They'll have it and for discount too. A lot of my customers go there."

The notion of getting away with the switch was like a carrot before a donkey. She wanted it so bad, she could almost taste it. Three hundred dollars should cover most of the cost of the suit, surely. She could make up the difference. She could put it on her credit card and have the insurance money before the bill came in. It would work. Taking the suit from the stand, she said, "I'll do it. Thanks, Nancy. Thanks for everything."

"I'll get the claim in right away."

Back in her car, Elaine raced down the Schuylkill Expressway into the city. Boyd's turned out to be a swanky place, with valet parking. Elaine threw her car keys at the attendant and raced for the entrance, lavender suit in hand. Inside, she halted and gaped in astonishment. The store was enormous, with a grand staircase and an escalator smack in the middle of it. She snagged the first salesperson she saw, a young woman.

"Help!" she exclaimed frantically, holding out the jacket. "The suit's color turned. I need the exact same one in gray, and I'm in a terrible rush. It's an Armani."

The woman frowned. "The Armani department is upstairs—"

"Take me there," Elaine said, grabbing her by the arm.

The poor bewildered saleswoman was hustled along, even as she led the way, taking in Elaine's urgency. In the designer department, row upon row upon row of suits greeted Elaine. Panic shot through her as she wondered how she'd find the one she needed. She was handed over to another saleswoman, who was told the problem. A miracle occurred when she led Elaine over to a rack. Several of the exact suit hung in pristine *gray* elegance on hangers. Elaine sobbed in relief. After a scramble to find the size on the old jacket and pants, they got a truly perfect match.

"Now you'll want tailoring," the woman began in her best professional voice.

"No, no!" Elaine said, thrusting her credit card at the woman. "I have no time for that. Just ring it up, please. I need this suit now!"

"But—"

"I *can't!*"

The woman frowned, shrugged, then rang up

the sale. She handed over the charge slip, saying, "Eight hundred and forty-five dollars—"

"Eight hundred and forty-five dollars!" Elaine burst out in shock.

"Yes. You won't find a better price. We're having a terrific sale on Armani at the moment."

Elaine couldn't believe what she was hearing. It was on sale! Nancy's offer didn't even cover half the price of the suit—and the damn thing was on sale!

She couldn't do it. She just couldn't do it. Even as she signed the slip like an automaton, she was telling herself she couldn't do it. Even as the suit was bagged, even as she left the store, even as she got into her car and drove home, she told herself she couldn't do it.

But she couldn't face Graham with the alternative: a lavender suit. She couldn't look stupid in front of him again, no matter how much it cost.

When she pulled up at her house, she realized she had only minutes to spare before Graham arrived. She dashed upstairs, passing Anthony with a quick hello and a query about his homework. After hiding the lavender Armani in the back of her closet, she took a plastic dry-cleaning bag from one of her dresses, pulled the revealing Boyd's bag and sales tags off the new suit, then put on the clear plastic bag.

"There," she said, satisfied that it looked exactly like a just-cleaned suit. "What do you think, Mikey?"

The cat in the middle of her bed didn't stir from his nap. She took it as a good sign. Then she thought of how her carefully worked-out budget had been shot to hell by an Armani, and her stomach immediately churned with anxiety and despair. Her notions of getting a new, much-needed washer had vanished with that gray Armani. Maybe Graham would be willing to come clean out the drain on a monthly basis. Now there was an intriguing notion . . .

"Mom! That guy from the game is here again."

"Okay." Elaine swallowed, knowing she had no time to toss her cookies now. She checked her appearance in her bureau mirror and tried to smooth down the few wisps of hair escaping from her scarf bow. Her makeup didn't look too bad, she thought hopefully, although she wished for time to renew her lipstick.

She took the suit and went downstairs on wobbly legs that she hoped didn't show. Anthony had a sulky expression on his face, while Graham's broke into a smile of pleasure that made everything worthwhile.

"Can I go to Steve's?" Anthony asked, already heading out the door. He didn't wait for an answer, but just shut the door behind him.

Elaine sensed a problem on her son's part and knew she'd have to deal with it later. Right now she had to deal with Graham. She held out the bane of her existence, her insides knotting from fear of discovery and the need to please. "Here's your suit."

"Looks great, just like new," he said, barely glancing at it as he took it from her. She blanched at his words. He went on, "How are you doing?"

"Fine," she lied. "Would you like some coffee or do you need to be somewhere tonight?"

"I have time." His smile widened. "I cleared my calendar in case you needed anything fixed."

She laughed in relief as she led the way to her nice neat kitchen. She'd stayed up an hour late cleaning it the night before, wanting no disasters to strike tonight. Of course, one had loomed anyway, but Graham had accepted the suit at face value. Thank goodness.

She firmly put monetary concerns out of her head. She'd live with her decision and lump it. But she knew who had learned the true lesson here, and it wasn't Anthony.

Graham hung the suit on the foyer closet door-knob before he followed her into the kitchen. She poured coffee for them both, using her good dishes and regretting that they were only decent stone-ware, not fine china. She carried over both cups and settled in across the small round table from him.

"No game tonight?" he asked, resting his head against the wall. He had shed his jacket and hung it on the back of the chair. His shirt was that pristine white silk he seemed to favor, made even whiter by the deep red of his tie.

She shook her head, not just in answer but in an

attempt to shake off her wayward thoughts. "A night off. I think I need it, and it's only April."

He chuckled.

They subsided into a companionable silence. She sipped her coffee, gazing at him as she did. She found she couldn't look away. Something about him pulled at her senses. He stared back at her, his gaze unwavering, almost smoldering. The coffee suddenly tasted like ashes in her mouth. She was imagining things, she thought as she tried to bring her wayward reactions under control. Even if he had kissed her twice, he really couldn't be attracted to her. Maybe she was just a challenge in that she was something different from the sophisticated women he was used to.

"Would you like cream?" she asked, belatedly realizing she hadn't put any out. She always forgot because she never used it herself.

"No," he said. "Like you, I only use one sugar. Did you have a good marriage with your husband?"

She nearly choked at the question. If she had been actually drinking her coffee, she wouldn't have been responsible for the results.

"I'm sorry," he said, making a face. "That was tactless of me. You don't have to answer it."

"That's okay. You just took me by surprise." Why, she wondered, did he want to know about her marriage? Did that mean he was seriously interested in her? Her heart began to beat faster. A logical part of her brain reminded her he couldn't possibly . . .

She realized he was gazing at her expectantly and cleared her throat, wondering where to begin and how to explain a marriage. "Joe was a wonderful man and a good father. He always brought home his paycheck and coached ball for Anthony. One night he went out for milk and bread and there was an accident."

She stopped herself, not because she was distressed but because she didn't know what else to say. She'd mourned her husband's death, but how could she explain the attitude of benign neglect that Joe had eventually developed toward her? She'd felt a slow withdrawal from him over the years, until it had turned into a restlessness on her part, a wondering if she'd missed something better. Whenever she'd tried to talk with Joe about it, he'd shrug her off with a "What did you expect?" answer. He was typical of other women's husbands that she knew, in that he came home every night and ignored his wife. People would have thought she was nuts to complain, so she never did. But Graham . . . She couldn't tell him all that. It wasn't his business for one thing, and she didn't want to sound like an ungrateful bitch for another.

"I'm sorry," he said, reaching across the table to cover her hand in sympathy. "I didn't mean to upset you."

The warmth of his fingers sent an awareness skittering along her nerve endings. She knew he meant to create a milder reaction than what she was feeling. She tried to control the tremor in her voice as she said, "You didn't."

His fingers began to stroke her skin, softly, gently, electrifyingly. "Have you been with anyone since?"

She dragged her gaze up to his, immediately mesmerized by their brown depths. "No." Her voice squeaked the answer. "No."

He smiled slightly, almost ruefully. "You're vulnerable emotionally."

"Like a time bomb," she agreed, trying to pull air into her lungs as his fingers never left off their deft stroking. Yet now they seemed more intimate and inviting. She tried to turn the tables. "What about you? Were you ever married?"

His fingers stopped. "Once. She couldn't handle the long hours I worked trying to keep my first store above water, or living in near poverty."

"You must have loved her very much, never to have married again," she said, regretting she'd found his vulnerable spot.

"You know, I don't think so," he replied thoughtfully, his fingers starting their stroking once more. "But it taught me a lesson that marriage and career don't mix."

Elaine felt breathless again. This whole conversation was getting out of hand, asking personal questions like this. She felt naive and foolish, but knew she wasn't finished as she said, "You're dangerous."

He smiled, almost wolfishly, but very intimately. "So are you."

God help her, but she felt as if she were melting inside. "Do you have any brothers or sisters?"

"No. Just my mother. You?"

"One brother and both my parents. They all live out in the Reading area."

He nodded almost absently. The room was silent . . . and filled with a tension so thick, she felt she'd need a knife to cut it away. His fingers exerted more pressure and focused in on the sensitive inside of her wrist. She hadn't known her wrist was an erogenous zone. He grasped her hand and tugged on it.

"Come here."

She shouldn't, she thought, but his hold was so steady and her will nonexistent. It was wrong, all wrong. As if in a dream, she felt herself rising from the chair and walking around the table to him. He pulled her down onto his lap, and a rush of desire swept through her body as she felt his hard thighs under hers. He stroked his fingers, those so knowledgeable fingers, along her jaw and neck, then brought her mouth to his.

Graham's head spun at the heady kiss. Elaine's lips could have been fashioned only for his, they fit so well. They matched his every movement before he even gave thought to it. A voice inside him scolded him for taking advantage of her in her current state. She *was* emotionally vulnerable, especially after talking about her husband. But Graham felt an unreasonable jealousy toward the man who'd known her so intimately. He liked it that he never knew what Elaine would do next, and he liked it that she made him laugh. He wanted those things to be special, just for him. He wanted her to be thinking about *his* kisses when she went to bed that night, not her late husband's.

Her tongue mated with his, and they rubbed together in a prelude to a more complete mating. Her body was warm and solid, her derriere nestled against his already hardening flesh. He caressed her shoulders, her throat, loving the little whimpers of pleasure that sounded from deep inside her. Her arms wound tightly around his neck, her nails digging slightly into his skin. Her breasts burned his chest, rubbing deliciously against him at her slightest movements.

Some sort of logic about right and wrong finally exerted itself in his brain, and he eased his lips from hers. Not entirely, for he couldn't stand that. "I'm taking advantage of you. I shouldn't."

"Probably not."

She sighed, her breath warm on his cheek. It sent another spiral of desire through him, then her lips searched his out for a second kiss that dissolved any notion of propriety on his part. His hand slid lower, finding her nipple already hard under the thin layers of blouse and bra. She moaned into his mouth when he rubbed his thumb around it. Sensations rocked him. She pressed her breast fully into his hand, and the kiss went wild. Hot, hungry, opened-mouth kisses followed one right after the other, until the air was filled with the sounds of gasps and moans and the rustles of clothing as eager hands slid over fabric. The scent of perfume and woman filled his senses. He couldn't think, he couldn't breathe, and it didn't matter. He only needed touch and taste to live on.

He wanted more than kisses with her, though. He wanted to touch her everywhere. He wanted to fill her with himself and feel her drive against him. He wanted the culmination of what they'd started.

Eventually he could no longer stand just touching her breasts and tasting her lips. At the same moment, she eased her mouth away from his, panting as if she'd run a hundred miles. He realized his own breath was ragged, and reluctantly let his hand slide away from the beautiful weight of her breast. They couldn't finish what they'd started, and they both had sensed it at the same time.

He kissed her forehead and temples, not ready to let go entirely the sensuality they'd created within each other. She pressed her face against his chest, and he cradled her in his arms.

"See?" he whispered. "You are dangerous."

He felt her smile. "I've never been dangerous in my life."

He chuckled. "Every second I'm around you is a big surprise, Elaine. Like now. Especially like now."

She didn't say anything, but he could easily feel her pleasure. He was digging himself in deeper with this widow, mother, schoolteacher, and he didn't care.

He ought to, a part of his brain told him, sending out a vision of Anthony. He ought to be sticking with unencumbered women whose expectations in a relationship didn't go beyond his own. He was so ill equipped to deal with children. He wondered if Elaine thought further about him than a few shared kisses. She probably wasn't any more ready to than he was.

But this was nice, he admitted, just sitting with a woman in the aftermath of explosive kisses. It was like being in school again, when a boy and girl were afraid to go further for all sorts of reasons and so settled for snuggling together, sharing short, mild moments of passion in between long moments of closeness. Maybe snuggling had gone out of fashion over the years, or maybe it was lost as one grew older. The only thing he knew was that it felt so good with Elaine, he wanted it to go on forever.

A little more wouldn't hurt, he thought, kissing her hair, the scent of flowers teasing his senses. "Would you have dinner with me Friday night?"

She ran her hand along his shirtfront, leaving a trail of sensual heat. "There's a game that night."

"Saturday, then." He rubbed her back, loving the feel of her spine.

Her hand caressed more strongly. "There's a game then too."

"Sunday."

"Another game."

He started laughing. Even though he ought to be annoyed or feel she was putting him off, he couldn't help seeing the humor in this. He didn't know of any woman who wouldn't go on a date because of a baseball game. "When *don't* the Phillies have a game?"

She lifted her head and grinned at him. "They go on the road beginning Monday."

He laughed all over again. "I can't. I have a business meeting."

She giggled. "Tuesday."

"Another meeting."

"Wednesday."

He roared with amusement, knowing what was coming. "It's my monthly dinner with my mother."

"Oh, Lord." She was laughing helplessly. "I'll skip that one."

"Thursday, then."

"The boys are back in town."

Suddenly this wasn't funny anymore. "If you don't want to have dinner with me, just say so."

She frowned at him, clearly bothered by his tone. "I would *like* to go out with you. You tell me when."

"Wednesday. I'll put my mother off until Thursday."

"You're a rotten son."

He raised his eyebrows. "Is that a no?"

"No. I'll be happy to go to dinner with you any day."

They both relaxed, smiling at each other. He pressed her shoulders and she settled back against him again.

"My mother's going to kill me," he muttered. She hated being put off even a day. He'd done it far too often over business.

"Sorry I won't be there for the murder. I'll be at the game."

He wondered what his mother would say if she knew he was rescheduling their dinner because of a woman this time. She'd probably turn cartwheels in the street. Him getting another wife was her latest campaign. His first marriage was so long ago and so short, he rarely thought of Janis. When he did, it was to wonder why he'd ever married her in the first place. His mother had been against the marriage, so why she wanted him to take the plunge again was mystifying. He didn't even want to think of what her opinion of Elaine, the soda-spilling, men's-room-invading maniac, would be.

His stomach growled at the same time he heard hers. They looked at each other and laughed.

"I think Wednesday just arrived," she said. "I have some Spam salad in the fridge."

"Spam salad?" How the hell did one make salad out of Spam?

"It's just tomatoes, hard-boiled eggs, some crunchy veggies all mixed in with macaroni and mayonnaise sauce."

"And Spam."

"Not elegant, but cheap, hearty, and pretty

good. This was hit-and-run meal night, so Anthony probably ate already." She made a face. "The child eats from the moment he comes home from school. I can't tell when snacks leave off and dinner starts."

Graham laughed. "You won't until he's about twenty-five."

"Thanks for the warning. So will you stay for dinner?"

"Sure. Who could resist Spam salad?"

"Not General Schwarzkopf, that's for sure."

She got up from his lap, but he caught her hand. She turned back, a puzzled expression on her face, and he tightened his fingers around hers.

"This doesn't forestall Wednesday's dinner," he said.

She smiled, looking almost shy yet very pleased. "Okay."

He let her go, and she fixed a dinner that didn't ignite her kitchen. But she had ignited him, against all of his common sense. Later he found the Spam salad everything she promised it would be.

He couldn't wait for Wednesday.

Elaine watched Graham leave from behind the window of her front storm door. As he drove away, she sighed with relief for a lot of reasons.

She still couldn't believe he was interested in her, and she'd been expecting him to take back the dinner invitation at any moment. Especially after she offered to feed him Spam salad.

Groaning at her menu, she shut the inside door and returned to the kitchen to start the dishes. How could she have offered him Spam salad? "Not elegant" wasn't even close in description. But he'd seemed to like it; he'd eaten two helpings.

And then there was the suit, another reason for a long sigh of relief. She probably should have confessed the truth, but oddly, it hadn't seemed like the right thing to do. Her stomach still churned when she thought about her credit card, but she'd worry about it when the bill came in.

Mostly, though, she sighed about their making out in her kitchen. Lord, but she was really having teenage flashbacks. If he hadn't stopped, she wondered if she could have. It felt so good to be held and kissed. And caressed. He sparked sensations in her that had been dormant so long, she couldn't remember if she'd *ever* felt them before. She hadn't wanted him to stop.

It would be so easy to fall for him, she thought. So damn easy.

The front door opened and closed, and she turned around to find her son on the threshold of the kitchen.

"Hi," she said, flushing a little at the thought of what he would have seen if he'd come home earlier. "I saw you had dinner. About half of it."

Anthony shrugged. "That guy gone?"

She nodded, although she knew he must have

seen Graham leave. He'd been outside playing soc-cer with the other kids. "Have all your homework done?"

"Yeah." Her son was silent for a moment, and she was about to turn back to the dishes when he said, "He's not coming back again, is he?"

She hesitated, sensing a strange tension in An-thony, then decided to tell him about next Wednesday. They both had to face it sometime, and she *had* talked to Anthony before about what would happen if she ever met anybody she wanted to date. Anthony should be somewhat prepared for this.

"Actually," she began, "I'm going out to dinner with him on Wednesday."

The expression on Anthony's face changed from sulky to pure hostility. "That's really stupid, Mom. He's a jerk."

"He's a nice man." She started to walk toward him, to offer comfort. "Anthony, we've talked about this before—"

Her son whirled and stormed up the stairs. A slamming door told her he'd barricaded himself in his room.

Elaine realized she had more problems with Graham than she'd first thought.

"Oh, brother," she muttered.

FIVE

After pulling on a fresh pair of jockey shorts and black socks, Graham rubbed his hands together in anticipation of dressing for his date with Elaine.

He'd worked like a madman all day so he could leave early, and even then he'd nearly been side-tracked by his comptroller. But he'd put the man off until tomorrow. He didn't even want to think about what his mother would say when he told her he'd be late for his dinner with her.

He entered his walk-in closet, quelling the urge to glance at his profile in the full-length mirror. What he didn't see couldn't shake his mind's version of his body. Besides, a man in jockeys and socks looked suspiciously like the star of a smoker movie. Nothing would kill his libido more than that. Facing his suits, he zeroed in on the one Elaine had had cleaned. He bet she'd like it if he wore it. Pulling off the plastic protector bag, he admitted Elaine's dry cleaner friend really did a great job. The suit looked so good, it actually gleamed with a crispness reminiscent of brand new.

He put on a pale pink shirt and clipped gold links into the French cuffs. The shirt amazed him each time he wore it, for the color somehow projected virility. He liked that. It was the image he wanted to project with Elaine. Feeling like a matador ready for his suit of lights, Graham unbuttoned the jacket, spreading out the sides in preparation for taking the trousers off their separate hanger.

He paused.

The trousers were unhemmed.

He blinked, then reached out and lifted the legs up to examine them closely. He ran his finger across the rough bottom edge, still not believing what he was seeing. Why would a dry cleaner take out hems to clean a suit? It didn't make a lick of sense.

He looked at the trousers more closely and realized the inside suspender buttons had magically reappeared. He hated suspender buttons because they always dug into his waist, and since he never wore suspenders he always had them removed. When he inspected the jacket, he saw the tailor's little signature stitching of his initials on the inside pocket was missing. He tried on the jacket and found the sleeves were a fraction of an inch too long. No matter how expensive a suit, jacket sleeves never fit his arms properly and always had to be adjusted. He put the pants on; the little changes that had made them a custom fit had also vanished. The unhemmed legs puddled around his feet.

"What the hell . . ." he muttered, staring at himself in the closet mirror. This was *not* his suit.

What had the dry cleaner done? The only logical explanation was that the dry cleaner must have given Elaine the wrong suit. He looked at his reflection again and chuckled wryly. Some poor guy probably had his by mistake.

Deciding to take a chance that the dry cleaners was still open, he stripped off the suit and hunted up the card Elaine had given him the night they'd met. He called the dry cleaner, Nancy, and was delighted when she answered the phone. A few minutes later he was very undelighted as he hung up.

What the hell had Elaine done?

Only one way to find out, he thought, and headed for his closet.

"Anthony."

Even though she was in a rush to finish the final touches of her dressing, Elaine raced out of her bedroom after spotting her son slipping down the hallway toward the stairs. She had been getting the cold shoulder from Anthony ever since she'd told him about her date. One more try, she thought, to smooth things over. "Anthony!"

The boy stopped and heaved a loud, clearly irritated sigh without turning around.

"I know you're a little upset about this," she began.

He whirled around. "I think it's disgusting! How can you go out on a date! What about Dad?"

Don't be defensive, Elaine warned herself, battling back the urge to do exactly that. "Anthony, we talked a long time ago, after your dad died, about how people have a need to be with those of their own age and experience. And about how those needs don't die when a partner does. We talked about it several times." She had wanted to prepare him, just in case she ever got asked out and decided to go. He had seemed to accept it then, but obviously accepting the abstract was easier than the reality. "You know I loved your father—"

"Ha!"

"And I love you very much," she finished firmly. "Just as you need to hang out with your friends, to talk and share things, so do I."

"Yeah." He sneered. "Just what are you gonna share?"

"You deserve to have your face slapped for that," Elaine said, angry but refusing to lose her control. "I'm not going to, because I haven't smacked you since you were four and you scared the hell out of me by trying to fly out your bedroom window while playing Superman. You're hurting right now, so I know you don't really mean this, but never speak to me that way again, Anthony. Never. I'm your mother, and I don't deserve it."

Her son looked stricken, and Elaine's anger collapsed. Tears welled in her eyes. "Anthony, honey, I love you very much, and *nothing* will change that. I'm only having dinner with Mr. Reed. It's just one date, so let's take it one at a time, okay?"

He nodded, although he still seemed upset.

She wondered if she'd gotten through to him at all. Anthony was more sensitive than he liked to let on. She knew he was of an age when his own sexuality was surfacing, giving him a lot of confusion to cope with. The thought of her son having a sexual nature shocked her as much as the thought of hers probably shocked, even repelled, him. Both of them had a lot of coping to do. Unfortunately, Anthony had to do the coping first.

She reached out and ruffled his hair in affection, about all he tolerated anymore and probably more than he wanted under the circumstances. "I love you, okay?"

He smiled a little. "Okay. I . . . I love you too."

She smiled. "Good. I needed to hear that. You heading to Steve's now?" He was staying with his friend while she went out.

He nodded again.

"Okay."

He turned to the stairs, then glanced back. "You look . . . nice."

"Thanks."

When she heard the door close behind him a few moments later, she hoped Anthony would grow comfortable with this as time went on . . . provided there was another time. She shivered, not sure she was ready for the way Graham always kept her emotions on a dangerous edge. She already felt way over her head with him, yet couldn't stop herself either.

She was just putting in her earrings when the doorbell rang. She gasped, glanced in the mirror, and immediately hated the black-and-white-checked silk dress she was wearing, with its splashes of vivid red, orange, and yellow flowers. Five seconds earlier it had been her best dress, but now it looked like something out of Barbara Bush's closet on a bad day. And each glance at her hair, her makeup, her stockings, even her shoes, elicited a groan of dismay.

The doorbell rang again.

Mumbling a curse, she grabbed her purse and headed down the stairs. Anthony had nothing to worry about. Graham would take one look at her and never go out with her again.

All worry melted away, however, when she opened the door and gazed into his face. Hell's bells, she thought dizzily, but he looked good with his dark features and sexy smile. At least he sent her senses off the charts.

"Hi," he said. He stepped inside and shut the door behind him.

"Hi," she croaked out, feeling like a tongue-tied schoolgirl on her first date.

His gaze swept over her. "You look beautiful."

She preferred to think he wasn't just being polite. What did she know anyway?

Through her dazed awareness, she noticed he was wearing the gray suit. It made him even sexier, she thought with pride as her gaze traveled lower, taking in the entire effect . . .

Right down to the pant legs that bagged at his ankles, draping over his gleaming black loafers.

Something hit her in the solar plexus as she stared in horror at his feet. How could the pants not be hemmed? How could they . . .

"Ready to go?" he asked.

She opened her mouth, but nothing came out of it. She was just too shocked.

He picked up her coat from the foyer coatrack. "This one?"

She nodded dumbly.

He helped her into it, then took her arm and led her out of the house. She wondered what the hell he was doing. He couldn't go like that.

"You know, your friend really knows how to clean a suit," he said, sending waves of anxiety through her. "It's like it's brand new."

"Brand new!"

He nodded. "Really an excellent job. I'll recommend her to Ed and his company. He knows most of the executives in the area."

She knew he knew this wasn't his original suit.

Any idiot would know it wasn't his suit! She remembered the saleswoman saying something about tailoring. No wonder she had. Why, Elaine thought, hadn't she listened? Why hadn't she *looked*?

Graham seated her in the car. "I was pleased I could wear the suit for you tonight. What do you think? I never saw a soda stain come out so well."

Why wasn't he yelling? Why was he acting as if nothing had happened? It occurred to her that he was goading her into explaining. Lord knows she needed to. She looked like an idiot yet again, despite all of her efforts otherwise. She wondered how far he would go if she didn't take the bait.

"Nancy did do a good job . . . didn't she?" Elaine stammered, trying to gather her thoughts. He was just shutting the door and it halted in mid-shut, the pause showing she had taken him by surprise. Maybe if she went along with his game . . . She glanced up at him. "I told you she would."

Graham blinked, then raised his eyebrows at her. "Yes," he said finally, "yes, you did."

Elaine nearly laughed. Well, if she was going down as a sinking ship, she was doing it in record speed.

He got in his side of the car, hitching up his pant legs in an exaggerated manner. Elaine asked, "Where are we going for dinner?"

"Le Bec Fin."

She groaned. That was the best restaurant in

Philadelphia. *She* wasn't dressed for it, let alone Graham.

"Anything wrong?" he asked, starting the car.

"I thought it took months to get a table there," she said suspiciously. He really couldn't mean for them to go to a world-class restaurant with his pants unhemmed. He truly had to be kidding. They were probably going to some nice Italian place where no one would look askance at his legs.

"I have connections."

"Oh." She tried to head him off, just in case. "I don't think I'm properly dressed for Le Bec Fin—"

"You look sensational. Stop worrying. Look, there's Anthony." He waved. Elaine waved like a robot.

Anthony, standing with his friends, a soccer ball in his hands, did not return the greeting.

"Maybe he didn't see me," Graham allowed politely.

"Anthony is having some trouble with his mother dating," Elaine said, knowing this was an honesty neither of them could fool around with.

"Oh."

Well, she thought. She had known she'd been expecting too much on this first venture back into Dating Land.

"I think I told you before," Graham said, "that kids and I don't mix."

"It's not you at all," she assured him. "He'd feel this way about any man. It's hard to lose your father at any time, but when you're an adolescent it's devastating. He just needs time to adjust to this."

Remembering Anthony's near temper tantrum, she hoped that was true. Nothing could be done to smooth the waters now, so she forced aside the guilt for the evening. Besides, she had other guilt to deal with at the moment. Suit guilt.

"I'm surprised he's not playing baseball," Graham said as he pulled out of her town house complex.

Elaine wondered if she should tell him he had just touched a sore spot. She found herself wanting to, suit guilt notwithstanding. "He'll play street ball, although tonight it's probably soccer because his friend is on the local team. But he won't play in the league games anymore, not since his dad died. They had had an argument about it that night. Joe was pushing Anthony to be on the traveling team, and Anthony didn't want to be. Then Joe went out to the store . . . and Anthony was left with a lot of guilt. I'm hoping he'll work his way through it and know the argument had nothing to do with it."

It occurred to Elaine that talking about a former husband in any form was probably a dating faux pas. But she came with emotional baggage . . . and he had asked.

"That's tough on a kid." Graham shook his head. "I lost my dad when I was twelve—"

"You did?" She gaped at him, surprised. She didn't know why she should be, because she really knew so little about him. But she wanted to know more—everything now.

He nodded. "It took me a couple of years to adjust. Like Anthony, I had a fight with my dad right before his heart attack. I don't know if I would have gotten over his death sooner if I hadn't, but all Anthony needs is time."

"You make me feel better," she said.

He smiled at her. "I'm glad."

She felt that sensuality rise up so quickly, it threatened to overwhelm her, urging her to throw herself into his arms. That wouldn't do, she thought. Not here, not now. But he was showing yet another side to himself for which she was unprepared.

When they drove across the bridge into center city Philadelphia, Elaine tensed, although she was still positive their ultimate destination was a nice serviceable restaurant. It wasn't until they left the car at a private parking lot on Walnut Street and were nearly in front of Le Bec Fin that she accepted the truth.

He was going to go through with it.

"Wait!" she said, stopping.

"We'll be late for our reservation—"

"You can't go like that," she said.

He grinned knowingly. "Like what?"

"I confess," she confessed, looking heavenward for help. "That isn't your suit. Can we go home now?"

"Elaine, I have one question for you. What the hell really happened to *my* suit?"

She turned her face away. "It turned purple during the dry-cleaning process—"

"Purple!"

She nodded. "Lavender actually. Nancy says it happens sometimes with silk. I couldn't tell you after all the fuss I'd made, so I bought you a new one."

"Elaine, I don't know your financial status, and I won't ask, but I doubt very much you could afford this. An Armani isn't cheap—"

"No kidding. It costs an Armani and a leg," she said in a lame joke.

He snorted. "Two Armanis and two legs. We'll straighten this out later. In the meantime we have a reservation."

"You've got to be kidding!" she exclaimed, wide-eyed. "You can't go in the restaurant like that."

He took her arm and hustled her forward the last few feet. "Let's see if they notice. And even if they do, I bet you ten dollars they won't throw me out. I wouldn't throw me out of one of my restaurants."

"You're crazy—"

But then they were inside the doors and surrounded by the reverent hush that seems to pervade all elegant four-star restaurants. Graham's reservation was confirmed with the maitre d', and they were directed to the bar. Their drink orders were taken, and they were assured their table would be ready in a "few minutes."

"We'll see," Elaine muttered, her gaze glued to his feet.

He leaned over from his bar stool and whispered into her ear, "Will you stop looking at my feet? People will think you have a fetish."

"No, that's you. The one with the need to balk social conventions." Despite her embarrassment, though, she found she was fighting for air at the way his breath had brushed warmly against her skin.

"One of us has to."

She was out of her depth with him, she thought, repeating the damnable truth she'd discovered practically since they'd met. But it was a truth she needed to listen to. He made things exciting, like a teenager pushing his way from childhood into rebellion. That's how she felt, she acknowledged. A little bit bad and very excited. Who would have thought unhemmed pant legs could have such an effect?

True to the restaurant's word, they were seated at a small intimate table a short time later, and had a leisurely, absolutely impeccable meal. A few more like this, Elaine thought, sopping up the last bit of raspberry cream from her torte, and his credit card bill would look like hers.

They talked, talked about everything from Cleo's penchant for teasing to Graham's mother's collection of pixies. Elaine found herself fascinated with the way his face lit up when he grinned. And the way he made her insides melt with one look. David Caruso could take lessons.

And no one noticed his pants.

As soon as they got outside, the laughter started. Elaine pulled a ten out of her purse and handed it over. "You won the bet. I can't believe nobody noticed. Or if they did, they were far too polite to say anything about it."

"You were the only pants fetishist in there." He took the ten from her, then slipped his arm around her waist, sending all kinds of signals through her body. They strolled along slowly, savoring the time together as much as they had savored the meal.

He finally broke the silence. "Now, tell me where you got the suit. I think I deserve to know."

"Boyd's."

He chuckled. "That's where I bought the first one."

"Maybe I should have asked for a discount."

He poked her in the ribs, and she twisted around, giggling. "You're fresh."

She came back against him, their hips bumping together and sending sensual messages through her veins. God, but she could really fall for this man. "Do you mean 'fresh' as in I'm neat, or 'fresh' as in just been plucked off the vine, or 'fresh' as in I've got a smart mouth?"

"I didn't know it was multiple choice." They had reached the parking lot and his car.

"Oh, yes. The kids in my class say 'fresh' when

they mean something's cool. My mother says 'fresh' when she means the apples were picked yesterday. Or I've got a smart mouth."

He leaned forward and kissed her thoroughly, pressing her back against the car door. It didn't matter that they were in a parking lot, with people passing just yards away on the sidewalk of busy Walnut Street. All that mattered was that his mouth toyed with hers, coaxing her tongue into a mating that had her wrapping her arms around his neck and hanging on for dear life. Her legs shifted, her thighs rubbing against his as she created a cradle for his hips. A shock of awareness coursed through her at the feel of his body so intimately pressed to hers. She wanted him so badly, her heart stopped with the power of it.

After long, long moments, he lifted his head. "Definitely a smart mouth. A very smart mouth."

"So is yours," she murmured.

He kissed her again, longer, hotter, and sweeter this time.

When he raised his head again, he said, "Let's go dancing."

She blinked. "Dancing!"

He grinned and nodded. "We can't make out here forever, much as I'd like to, and I want to feel your body against mine. Dancing."

She nodded, understanding him completely. She might want him, but she wasn't ready for sex, not emotionally anyway. But dancing . . . dancing was all part of the process of being courted. She hadn't danced in years and years, and she wondered if she remembered how.

"Your pants!" she said, suddenly remembering them.

"It'll make things interesting," he replied, opening the door and nudging her inside. His hand was on her hip, burning through the material of her dress.

As soon as he shut her door, Elaine took a deep, deep breath.

Dancing. Oh, boy.

She was pressed against him, her left arm draped across his shoulder, her fingers toying with his collar, while her other hand lay nestled in his palm, drawn close to their sides. Her head fit perfectly into the curve of his neck as they swayed together to some slow tune Graham didn't recognize and didn't care that he didn't. His senses were filled with the light, flowery smell of her shampoo. The backs of his fingers brushed along her breast, a torture he happily endured.

She lifted her head and smiled slowly, sensually. "I've always loved this song, even though it's sad. 'But Not for Me.'"

"What's not for you?" he asked vaguely, his lips inches from the soft flesh just under her ear. So white, he thought, like silk. It would be sensitive, and if he pressed his lips to it, she would curl her shoulder up in the most delicious way . . .

She nudged him, laughing. "Nothing's not for me. The name of the song is 'But Not for Me.' Graham, where are you?"

"Hell, I don't know, but don't bring me back," he murmured, giving into his urge. His lips touched the soft, soft flesh, and she shivered and turned her shoulder up just as he'd imagined. But he hadn't thought of the shiver. His fantasy had missed the best part.

"Has it become hot in here?" Her voice was a whisper.

"It's been steaming for me for a long time." He swung her around on the floor . . . and nearly tripped on his pant legs.

That broke the spell.

Elaine collapsed against him, shaking with laughter. "When are you going to give this up with the pants?"

"I don't know." He rubbed her back, laughing too.

"How about now? It's getting late and you have a long drive home."

Much as he wished he didn't, Graham thought. Tonight had been fun, even silly at times, and he didn't want it to end. Elaine had a demanding job, though, and probably needed to make an early night of it. And she was right that he had a long drive. Because he couldn't stay over. Neither of them was ready for that. "I give up under protest," he said. "But I don't want a broken leg, either."

They gathered her coat from the coat check at

the dance club and headed for her house. It wasn't too far. And that was unfortunate, Graham thought when he glanced over and caught her with a dreamy half smile on her face.

He couldn't remember the last time he'd enjoyed himself this much, then immediately amended it to the last time they'd been at a ball game, and the night her house had practically fallen down around their ears, even that first night they'd met. Elaine had him doing things he never thought he'd do. She could take a Roman man's *dignitas* and shred it beyond repair in a matter of moments—and leave him laughing. She didn't even mean to do it, either.

She did a lot of other things to a man when she melted against him the way she did. But there were problems, major problems, that he tended to forget whenever he got around her. What she'd said about her son earlier disturbed him, as much as he could sympathize with Anthony's trouble. He shoved the thoughts aside, not wanting to deal with their implications.

"Will you be at the game tomorrow night?" he asked, then chuckled. "Dumb question."

"True. And you're going to your mother's, remember?"

He grinned. How could he forget? When he'd told her he couldn't come for dinner that Wednesday, his mother had begun a lecture on working too hard, then immediately switched to congeniality and avid curiosity when he told her he would be on a date. His mother would like Elaine, he bet. But their meeting had a connotation he wasn't ready to face.

"Cleo, Jean, and Mary wouldn't let me off anyway," Elaine went on. "I'm the chauffeur."

"You pick them all up?" He didn't understand his fascination with her relationship with the three older women—except they made him laugh too. He wondered what he would do if they had been thirty years younger. Kill himself out of the sheer pleasure of their company, probably.

"It's not that bad," she said, referring to her chauffeur job. "Jean's in the Fairmount Park area, Cleo's in West Philadelphia, and Mary's in South Philly. It's only about twenty minutes more . . . if the traffic's with me."

He shuddered. "I'll bet most of the time it's not."

She shrugged. "I don't mind."

"I think you ought to get a medal."

"I think you ought to," she countered, grinning. "You've sat in front of them for two games."

He reached across the console and took her hand. The warmth of it sent his blood surging. "I think you're the medal. And the curse, when you're armed with soda."

She chuckled in a way that said pure sex. "I was a good girl tonight."

"Very good." Damn-near-killed-him good, he thought.

Dating her was very dangerous. He knew he shouldn't continue, not with all his concerns about her son, and especially not with her son not liking his mom dating.

One dinner date, he told himself. Just this one.

SIX

"So are you going out with him?"

Anthony asked the question with a tone of voice that said he didn't intend to like any answer but no. Elaine gazed at him, leaving off her finishing makeup touches before they left for the Sunday game. How was she supposed to handle this whole dating business? Anthony was still sulking over her first date with Graham.

"Let me ask you something," she said. "If I didn't date him, would you like him? Honest answer."

Anthony, who had been leaning on her bedroom doorjamb, started fiddling with the door catch, effectively turning his head away as he pondered her question. Finally he looked up and said, "I suppose I'd like him. I guess. I don't know."

"Then how can you not like him just because he's asked me out?" she asked logically.

"Forget it!" her son snapped, spinning around and heading down the hall.

"That was well done," she muttered to herself in disgust.

It didn't matter anyway, she admitted as she followed her son out of the bedroom and down the stairs. Anthony had nothing to worry about. Graham hadn't called since Wednesday night. Granted, he'd been at his mother's on Thursday and she'd been at the ballpark every night since, but she had an answering machine. It had been conspicuously empty of messages from one Graham Reed.

She checked on Mikey's food and water dishes, which were fine, then patted the cat on the head as he cried piteously to try to get the food dish topped off. Anthony was already at the car, she noted. Their game "necessities" were missing from the kitchen table.

She was about to go out the front door when the phone rang. She scrambled to answer it, yanking the receiver to her ear before the third ring. "Hello?"

"Elaine? You sound breathless."

Disappointment surfaced at the sound of her mother-in-law's voice. "Hi, Esther. I was just going out the door, that's all."

"I thought I was cutting it close before you had to leave for the game. Joe Senior and I wanted to have Anthony over next weekend. We know the Phillies will be on another road trip then."

Elaine smiled. Her in-laws had the baseball calendar down pat. "It's fine with me, but I'll ask him. How about if I call you back tonight?"

"Fine."

They chatted a few minutes more before she hung up. She locked up the house and went out to the car. Her five-year-old Chevy was a strong contrast to Graham's luxurious Mercedes, with its supple leather seats and car phone. She unlocked the trunk for Anthony, who was waiting to dump in their stuff. He didn't say a word to her.

"Grandma Esther just called," she said. "They want you to come over next weekend. Do you want to go? I told her I'd call her back tonight."

"Yeah. Yeah, okay."

She knew he wanted to keep up his ties with Joe's parents, and that was good. Maybe it would be good, too, for her and Anthony to have a weekend apart. Maybe Anthony would get used to the notion of her dating if he had a little time to think about it without her around.

She might as well put him out of his misery and tell him the truth about Graham. No matter that he could turn her upside down with a touch, Graham Reed, to borrow a baseball phrase, was out of her league. Way out. He hadn't called, and he *still* hadn't given her his number. He was telling her the same thing. She tried to ignore the pain that squeezed at her heart. What was she getting so upset for anyway? This wasn't high school, where everyone acted like they were engaged after the first date. She was an adult and so was Graham. It had only been some flirtation and one date. She'd better start acting as if that were the case.

But he had been fun and funny. He had made her laugh.

After her son shut the trunk lid, she put her hand on his arm, stopping him from getting in the car just yet. "I doubt Graham will ask me out again, Anthony. But just because he was a one-date thing, that doesn't mean I won't get asked out by another man. And I may want to go. I love being a mom, being your mom especially, but I'm a human being too. I can't turn off those needs because your dad died—"

"I don't want to hear this," Anthony said.

"You'll hear it," Elaine snapped, losing her patience. "You have to accept that I'm a person, too, just like you. You're going to begin dating soon, you probably like a girl already. You better hope I accept your need to be with a girl a whole lot better than you're accepting mine to be with a man. Now, we're going to go the ballpark and we're going to root and scream for the Phils and we're going to have a damn good time doing it. Do I make myself clear?"

A smile flickered around Anthony's mouth.

Elaine grinned back at him. The tension of a moment ago deflated in their amusement. She put her arm around his neck and gave him a quick hug before he could stop her. "Come on. Let's go watch baseball, babe."

"Mom!"

She laughed at his outrage until even he was laughing as he protested her teasing. It was a start to accepting loss, she thought. No matter how much it hurt.

Inside the ballpark Elaine's first glance went to the seats in their section. The row in front of their own was conspicuously empty. The Phillies were playing the Braves again, though it had been only a little more than a month since the opening series. She couldn't believe that was all the time that had passed since she'd first met Graham. It seemed so much longer, as if he'd had months and months to embed the taste, touch, and smell of him into her brain.

"Do you think Jane will fall asleep again?" Jean asked as they all climbed the stairs together to their seats. "She did at that game last year, remember? Right there behind home plate in those special seats."

"Old Ted boy must be keeping her awake in extra innings," Cleo said, cackling raucously at her own joke.

"How could she fall asleep in the best seats in the house?" Mary asked. Clearly she expected no answer, for she went on, "I would have traded her if she didn't want to watch the game, no matter how good she looks on those exercise videos of hers."

"I'm sure she'd have gone for that," Elaine said.

"We could have traded Cleo for her, and Ted would have died a happy man, right, Cleo?"

"Get your mind up to the gutter where it belongs, child," Cleo scolded. "Although he couldn't get no better than me."

Everyone laughed. Anthony just shook his head, as if they were all batty today. There, Elaine thought, normal baseball gossip, and she was participating. It felt good. It meant life went on without dates and men. That her breasts still ached for his touch, and her body still pulsed with unfulfilled need, only meant the physical attraction was running a few days behind her common sense.

She took her usual seat proudly, deliberately putting her foot on the empty seat in front of her. The men who really made her heart pound and her body thrum would be taking the field in a little while. To hell with "suits" and their suits. Life was back to normal.

Just as the game was starting, her life skittered back into chaos. The hairs on the back of her neck rose a second before she spotted Ed Tarksas and his "client" emerging from the concourse entrance below.

"My God," she murmured, sucking in her breath.

What the hell was Graham doing there on a Sunday afternoon?

She immediately snatched her foot off the seat back, forgetting her determination to keep it there the entire game in a gesture of mental defiance, even if it turned blue and fell off.

"Looks like the suits are back," Jean said in a low voice.

Anthony stiffened. He turned to look at Elaine as if it were her fault that Ed and Graham were there. She wanted to protest that she and he had held season tickets to every game for the last umpteen years, but any logic with Anthony would just be wasted.

Graham and his advertising man made their way along their row. Ed nodded at them in acknowledgment. Graham said, "Hello," in a general way. They sat down. Shocked, Elaine stared at Graham's back as all the things he should have said raced through her mind. He never said a word to her, though. Not one word.

The message had been so very clear.

The pain she had been suffering earlier was nothing compared to what she felt at this snub. Why? she wanted to ask him. What was wrong with her? Everything, she acknowledged. From the extra ten pounds and ten years, to, no doubt, her financial base, or lack of it. A part of her brain, probably that damnable common sense again, reminded her that she had absolutely no reason to think that of him, that they had acted coolly before while in their seats. Her brain even pointed out that maybe he was worried about *her* reaction to him.

Fool, she thought murderously at herself.

"Mom? Are you okay?"

She focused on Anthony, who had a look of concern on his face. Her son's gaze slid sideways, toward the two men in front of them. Or rather one man in particular. It was nice to know her son had seen the snub and hadn't liked it. She wondered how he would reconcile it with his aversion to her dating Graham. She could feel the three older women closing the slight spaces between them all, as if in support. Forcing a true smile for her son's sake, she said, "I'm fine."

Anthony frowned at her, but didn't say anything further.

The national anthem was sung and the first ball was thrown out. Elaine, however, found her concentration for the game completely gone. That was a first, she admitted ruefully. Her awareness of Graham was knife-edge keen and very bitter. He and Ed chatted or watched the game, clearly both of top concern to Graham. She sat in her seat for three innings before finally surrendering to the need to get away.

Even as she excused herself she refused to run or show her hurt. She left for the ladies' room with dignity . . . and once she got inside a stall, she leaned her head against the stall door and drew in a deep, hurting yet cleansing breath.

"I'm okay, I'm okay," she muttered over and over to herself.

When she finally calmed down, she knew she had been silly. In fact, she'd made a few sparks of lust out to be some kind of kismet. *Grow up*, she told herself, straightening. She'd go back out there, be friendly, and expect no more. That was the mature thing to do.

The moment she left the ladies' room, all her good intentions were shot to hell. Graham stood against the privacy wall, clearly waiting for her. Her heart beat faster in hopeful anticipation.

"Hi," he said.

He had come down after her and he had said hello. Maybe it was better than she'd thought. She smiled. "Hi."

He didn't smile back. Instead he looked earnest. She wasn't sure if she liked earnest. "I'm sorry I haven't called you, but I had an emergency at the office."

She smiled wider in relief. Of course. He had had trouble at the office and hadn't had a chance to call. Even though she had thought of that possibility and dismissed it, she should have trusted that that was the case. He was here at the game, a clear indication that he had wanted to see her the first chance he had. After all, he hated baseball and didn't like any of the advertising proposals Ed Tarksas had made so far. Why else would he be there, but for her? She felt better already.

He cleared his throat. "I wanted to talk to you privately. I'm . . . this is hard to say . . . I'm having some misgivings about our relationship."

All her bright hope crashed to the ground. Elaine sucked in her breath. "What misgivings?"

He made a poor attempt at a shrug, as if they were minor. She knew already that they weren't. "Elaine, I care about you a lot. You must know that." He paused, clearly waiting for her to make some kind of acknowledgment. She didn't. He continued. "You have a child, and I have a high-pressure job. I'm not sure I can devote the time you and Anthony would require—"

"I see." She couldn't stop her next words. "I've got emotional baggage you don't want."

"It's not like that," he said, grimacing.

"Of course it is. If I didn't have a child, would you be having this conversation with me or would you be asking me to dinner again?"

He hesitated, a dead giveaway to his feelings.

"Ha!" she exclaimed triumphantly. "Very well. Fine then. I had a nice time the other evening. Dinner was lovely, so I'll be going now."

She put power to words and headed for the concourse exit. Dignity, she thought, while forcing away the lump forming in her throat. She was doing this with dignity.

Dodging around several groups of people, Graham raced to catch up with her before she made it into the stadium. He hadn't wanted to talk with her over the telephone, and this had seemed like the best place to him. Instead he'd made a mess of it. Cursing his lack of tactfulness, he took her arm, bringing her around to face him.

When he looked into her eyes, he felt the shock of his attraction to her rising up inside him. Her scent invaded his senses, reminding him acutely of the way she'd felt in his arms when they'd danced together. Of the way her lips had felt under his. He wanted her desperately, and he was letting her go.

"I'm not saying this right, and I'm sorry." His brain scrambled for a better explanation than what had taken him three days to come up with and had failed so miserably. "Elaine, I really care about you, but I'm not good with children. You saw how that kid in the men's room was that time. You know Anthony doesn't like me much. He probably doesn't like me at all."

She didn't answer him. He didn't think she could because he was right and she knew it.

"I don't want to do this. I don't." He had never meant anything more in his life. "Yet it's not fair to you to begin something we can't finish."

"Don't hide behind my son, Graham. Anthony would object to anyone I dated right now. You lost your father, so you know it's true. You probably felt the same with your mother. I was a little different for you, not some bimbo with brains smaller than her boobs, which is probably your usual fare. Don't worry, I'm not in any way crushed beyond repair. I'm just sorry I expected more from you than you are capable of giving."

"Elaine, you're misunderstanding me entirely." He actually began to pull her into his arms, then stopped himself.

"Where am I misunderstanding you?" she asked sweetly.

"I'm just not good with children. Anthony's at a delicate stage in accepting his dad's death, and I just don't think I'll handle it well. In fact, I know I'm incapable of it. He needs stability, and I can't offer that, not with a business that takes twenty-five hours a day to run. I don't want to scar him. How fair is that to him? And how fair is it to you if we go out a few more times, get in deeper with each other, and *then* are forced to accept the inevitable? It's better to do it now, Elaine. For you and Anthony."

She seemed to deflate, her body shrinking in upon itself as her shoulders slumped and she hung her head. "I know you're probably right, Graham. Yes, I'm attracted to you, I admit it. But from the beginning I didn't think this would work out. You're just being sensible. And fair to all of us."

Somehow he didn't like it that she thought things wouldn't work out between them, even though he felt the same. He put that thought aside. This was one of the hardest conversations he'd ever had. His heart ached from hurting her . . . and hurting himself. When he'd left her last Wednesday night, he hadn't had any doubts. His visit with his mother and the supply crisis that he'd had to cope with, though, had kept him from calling her. In the back of his mind the doubts about his ability to deal with her son had surfaced and begun to grow. Finally he'd accepted what he had to do and that was to end this before anyone was hurt. It didn't matter. He hurt anyway.

"Friends?" he asked in the age-old tradition of breakups everywhere. It sounded like the pap it was, and he hated himself for even saying it.

"Oh, sure," she replied in a carefree tone that knifed through him. She actually smiled.

He hated her for that.

"I'm going to go up," she said. "I don't want to miss any more of the game than I have to."

She went out into the stadium without a backward glance.

Graham cursed fervently under his breath, every bone in his body crying out that he'd just made the biggest mistake of his life. What the hell was the matter with him? He'd done the right thing by her, the right thing for her son, and even for himself. So why did it feel like the wrong thing? None of it made any sense.

He dragged himself out into the stadium, glancing down to the action on the field. The players stood in their positions as if frozen while they waited for the windup and the pitch. He felt about as frozen as they looked. The pitcher kicked up his leg, then hurled the ball like a streak of white lightning over the plate. The batter swung and missed. Suddenly everybody was moving as the teams changed defensive and offensive positions.

Graham sighed, then turned toward the long climb up the stairs to his row. The concrete steps looked three times as wide as they were. He didn't glance up, not wanting to see her before he had to. He made it to his row after endless seconds and squeezed past people in a kind of slow-motion film sequence.

"Hey, Mr. Suit," Cleo called out. "How'd you like the way Greene fanned that last batter?"

"Pretty good." He couldn't help smiling at her, blessing her for breaking the tension growing inside him. He looked at Elaine finally. She was staring intently at the field. If she felt his gaze, she didn't show it. Anthony was watching the game too. Why couldn't the kid have liked him? He might have been willing to try then.

But the three widows were definitely more interested in him than the game. Six pairs of knowing eyes watched him take his seat.

Some of Ed's colleagues were in the company block of seats, apparently taking advantage of them to see a Sunday ball game rather than do business. He was the only business client as far as he could gather. Some business client, he thought. He might as well make it worth Ed's time, because he had never felt more like a fraud.

Aware of every inch of Elaine at his back, he said to Ed, "I know it's a Sunday, but I'd like to look over those sketches you sent to my office. Can we stop in there after the game instead? I think I want to look at them today."

"Sure," Ed said. "We can leave any time you want. Even now."

Graham nodded. "Fine. Let's go, then."

❦━━━━━❦

Six days later Graham knocked on Elaine's door.

She opened it. Her expression changed from exasperation to shock in a blinding instant.

Graham drank her in, drank in the perpetual ponytail that he liked so much, drank in her breasts outlined under her cotton blouse, drank in her tight, faded blue jeans over a figure that rivaled Marilyn Monroe's. She was no young girl, but all woman, and he had missed her terribly.

"I don't know why I'm here," he said, waiting for her to slam the door in his face. "I don't know why I'm here . . . except that I couldn't stay away from you."

SEVEN

Elaine didn't say anything, she just stared at Graham.

It had taken nearly a week before she'd finally begun to come out of the funk that had set in over this man. Anthony's visit to his grandparents that weekend was allowing her the peace and quiet she needed to settle over her like a soothing cloak.

The cloak had just been ripped away.

"Elaine, please," he said. "Can we talk about this?"

She found her voice finally, but it was only enough to say inane things. "Graham. Why are you here?"

"Hell, I can't explain . . ." He ran his hand through his hair. "Elaine, I haven't felt right since last week. I had to see you again."

He had been man enough to say he had problems, she thought, which was good. He had hurt

her, which was bad. But she had hurt herself over-
all, having had stars in her eyes, to use the old
phrase. The damn thing was true, unfortunately.
She still hurt a little, and in another truth, she still
wanted him badly.

He looked good. In his gray suede jacket and
jeans, he looked far more sophisticated than a man
she had a right to be around. So why was he here,
with a woman pushing forty who shopped at JC
Penney on her best day?

Maybe he wanted a better crack at the way he'd
handled the breakup for his pride's sake, she
thought. Well, she'd stop this before it started.
"You don't have to feel guilty about anything, Graham—"

"I don't feel guilty, dammit!"

She stepped back, startled at his forcefulness.
His fingers closed over hers on the door frame.
Elaine sucked in her breath as his touch sent her
senses spinning. She'd been stupid to think she was
in control of anything around this man, let alone in
control of him.

"Please." His voice was quieter, gentler. "Can I
come in and talk?"

She hesitated, then moved back a few more
steps, giving him entry. He strode inside, pushing
the door shut behind him. His presence seemed to
turn her small foyer into a tiny box. He looked at
the cloth in her hands.

"I was dusting," she said lamely.

"Oh." He glanced around, then back at her.

"Elaine, I can't explain why I'm here, except it feels right. I thought I would feel better just seeing you, and I do. Maybe I got cold feet, cold everything for a moment, after we went to dinner."

Some part of her brain began to function again. *"You feel better.* Does this mean you have suddenly reversed yourself and that all your trepidations about dealing with children, especially my son, are nonexistent?"

"No." He shoved his hands in his jacket pockets and sighed. "I'm still scared as hell about your kid, but I'm willing to try."

She shook her head. "I don't think so, Graham—"

He put his hands on her arms, his fingers closing around her flesh like bands of iron and sending all kinds of messages through her already vulnerable system. She couldn't resist the physical attraction she had for him. She didn't want to.

"Elaine, let's try."

"We shouldn't—"

His mouth covered hers, opening her lips for his tongue to touch, to savor her own. She melted against him, her resistance gone. The dust cloth fluttered from her limp fingers. She just needed to touch him, to have him touch her once more.

He pressed her back against the wall, his body settling against hers in the most satisfying of ways. She wrapped her arms around his neck, threading her fingers through his hair, the strands like roughened silk. The kiss went on for endless minutes, just the sounds of their mouths locked together, their heavy breathing filling the silence.

"We shouldn't," she whispered, when they both finally came up for air. Her hands kneaded the muscles at his shoulders, belying her words.

"Maybe not," he said, than ran his tongue along the sensitive skin under her ear. "Where's Anthony?"

"At his grandparents'." She could barely think straight. "For the weekend."

He made a noise in the back of his throat and brought his mouth back down on hers, his tongue thrusting inside to mate with her own.

She shuddered at the sensations he was creating inside her. He kissed her again and again, long, frantic, driving kisses that had her head spinning and her body restless. She was being swept along in a sudden outpouring of desire even as she swept him in with her.

Gasping for breath, he eased his mouth away and leaned his forehead against hers. She couldn't find the will to open her eyes. Their lips met for a lingering kiss . . . then a second and a third. His fingers toyed with the buttons of her shirt, pushing the first one through, then the next. Slowly the upper curves of her breasts were revealed, his fingers just brushing against her flesh. She watched his hands, fascinated with the dark hairs dusting the back of them, fascinated with how they moved with such sureness. She'd never realized before how much a man's strength and virility could be revealed in his hands.

After he undid the last button, he slowly spread open her shirt. Her breath came quicker. Her thoughts were a jumble of feminine pride at having a man admire her body and fear that it wasn't good enough to truly arouse him. The latter was winning out when he lowered his head and reverently kissed the upper flesh of her breasts revealed by her bra. Nothing could have dispelled her insecurities quicker or better than that act of need.

She ran her fingers through his hair and pressed his face to her, not wanting him to stop. He growled in the back of his throat and pushed her bra away, then took a nipple, dark from childbearing, into his mouth. His wet tongue lapped and swirled around the hardened tip, and her need roared back like a freight train on an unstoppable course. She cried out in pleasure, clutching at him and tearing at his jacket, the expensive suede taking the punishment as she stripped it from him. His shirt was silk, but she yanked it up, the buttons coming free despite her awkward grappling. Finally she had what she wanted and needed so badly, and that was to feel his skin under her hands.

She explored him, finding the way his muscles seemed to ripple under her palms. The hair on his chest was silky and soft, not at all what she'd expected, and it tickled her sensitive skin. He wasn't young-man skinny, and that suited her. Instead he was solid hard flesh that made her body yield to his.

He undid her bra, pushing it and her shirt away from her, leaving her upper body exposed. His hands and mouth were real on her flesh, touching, tasting, wanting. She needed it so badly, needed to be needed by another in the most basic way of humans. She needed to be sexual again. And with Graham she felt like the most incredible sexual woman created, for with every touch and kiss he conveyed a desperate need for her. He could have gone to any other woman, but he had come back to *her*.

A part of her brain reminded her of all the obstacles he was ready to throw in their path, that just because he'd come back didn't mean he'd stay. She accepted the concerns and accepted whatever she could have for this short time. She would worry about dealing with her son when he came home— and if Graham was still around.

She pushed aside her qualms as he straightened. His chest caressed hers, crushing her breasts against him, skin to skin. It had been so long for her, so long.

"You feel so good," he whispered, pressing kisses on her ear and neck. "So good."

"Come to bed with me," she said.

Everything ceased abruptly, as if time were suspended in that instant. He raised his head. "Are you sure?"

"Yes." She nuzzled his chest, the hairs tickling her lips. His skin was so warm and he smelled so good, she thought. Sandalwood and male. "Yes. I'm very sure."

Taking his hand, she led the way to her bedroom upstairs, leaving behind the first of their clothes. He walked slightly behind her, and she could feel his gaze on her bare back. She glanced down self-consciously at her breasts, yet couldn't help but feel sensual at the same time.

Halfway up the steps he pulled her back against him, his hands covering her breasts.

"Do you know what it does to a man when you're like this?" he asked, his voice raspy.

"No." She laid her head on his shoulder and pressed her bottom against his already hardened body. She closed her eyes and shuddered. "No. Show me."

With a growl he spread little, almost biting kisses on her shoulder, his hands kneading her soft breasts, palms rubbing along the sensitive tips. Elaine moaned and sagged against him, her legs like jelly at the incredible need he was creating inside her. He took her weight easily. She brought her hands up over his, feeling his fingers caressing her flesh. The pressure built up inside her until she thought she would explode with it.

"Your bedroom," he prompted.

The words penetrated. Somehow she got herself the rest of the way up the stairs, even though her hands never let go of him. A while back she'd done over her bedroom in colors of mauve and green, stacking the bed with bolsters and ruffled pillow covers, marking the entire room as female territory. Now the male had come into it, looking for the passion and the vibrancy of the woman who slept there each night.

The door didn't even get closed behind them. Graham turned her around in his arms, and they fell back together on the bed, their mouths already feeding off each other in a frenzy of escalating passion. The rest of their clothes were shed in a jumble of fumbling hands that afterward smoothed over flesh and muscle with mature experience. She touched him everywhere, loving the feel of hair-roughened male skin, loving the feel of solid male weight pressing her down into the mattress as he lay half over her, loving encircling him and stroking him to insanity. His hands seemed to delight in finding each little spot that elicited a moan of desire from her. Her hips bucked against him as he stroked her intimately. She had been married for a long time and had enjoyed lovemaking with her husband, but this was all so new and fresh, she again felt like she was a teenager once more—only better. So much better.

She urged him to her, wanting him so badly, she couldn't stand it any longer. He pushed himself inside her slowly until she sheathed him. Wrapping her legs around his hips, she took him even more deeply into her. His muscles tensed for a long second, and they began to move together, adjusting to the rhythm and need for each other. Elaine thought she would die from the heat rising inside her. Her urgings quickened, and she dug her nails into Graham's shoulders, clinging to him as the only real thing in the storm of her emotions.

At the very moment when she could stand no more, a huge pulsing wave washed over her, pulling her deep into a velvet blackness that stopped heart and mind. Graham buried his face in her throat and thrust one last time into her, flooding her with his warmth. She took him in, wanting nothing more than to feel his satisfaction mingle with her own.

Slowly normalcy surfaced and she became aware of Graham's weight growing heavier on her body and the cool air circulating over her naked flesh. No regrets, she thought. Whatever happened next, she would have no regrets for this moment.

He raised his head and smoothed her hair back with gentle hands. He smiled at her. "Are you all right?"

She smiled back. "Oh, yes."

He kissed her nose. "I just wanted to make sure. No regrets?"

"No." Then questions she should have thought of long before abruptly surfaced.

"You're not all right," he said, some of her dismay clearly in her expression. "What? What's wrong?"

"I—I suppose I should have asked you a few things about your past before we . . ." She closed her eyes, thinking how little she knew about his past life beyond his short marriage. "And I should have used protection, even though this just happens to be a time of the month when I shouldn't get pregnant. And we should have discussed any health concerns . . . I'm not very good at this. All the rules have changed since I was last single."

"I haven't been with anybody in a long time," he said, answering her most disturbing question. "Almost a year. And I had myself tested afterward, and I'm in perfect health. The rules changed on me, too, and I'm too damn old to cope with them, I think." He grinned. "I have to admit I didn't think about some of the old rules either. Are you sure you can't get pregnant?"

She started to giggle, thinking they were like kids, all passion and no caution. "I shouldn't take it lightly, but I was feeling like a teenager, and pregnancy was the biggest panic back in those days. Yes, I'm sure it's a good time. I had trouble conceiving Anthony, and I had to go through a rigorous checkup of my body functions so I would know when was the best time and when wasn't. Lord, this sounds so clinical, doesn't it?"

He shook his head. "You make me feel like a teenager too. I can't wait to get my hands on you, and I forget all good sense the moment I do."

"I'm not complaining," she murmured.

He started to move off her, but she tightened her legs along his sides. He grinned.

"Now that we've got all the health class out of the way," he said, "we can get onto the good stuff."

She ran her hands down his arms. "What's that?"

He sucked in his breath. "If you keep doing that, I'll forget everything again."

"Really?" She trailed her fingertips along his biceps.

"Yup." He kissed her lingeringly. It turned from one kiss to two to three . . . to more. Just deep, deep kisses that satisfied the heart and soul.

They were so intimate, so comforting, she thought, her body absorbed in the sensations they created. If she'd needed anything to reassure her that he found her attractive and that he wanted to be with her, it was this.

She felt so connected to him that she wanted to tell him all the things about herself she never shared with anyone else. The urgings rode up inside her until she could no longer ignore it. "Graham, you told me about your marriage, but I never really told you about mine."

He paused in his nuzzling.

She went on. "My marriage wasn't an unhappy one, but it wasn't a happy one either. We were never madly in love. Eventually Joe developed an attitude of benign neglect, and the more he did, the more restless I became for something more."

"I don't know how anyone could be complaisant about you," Graham said, kissing her. "I could never be."

He even said the right things, she thought, and

surrendered her emotions to this man who evoked them with one look.

Eventually the desire rose again between them, more leisurely this time, giving way to long, concentrated explorations. When the final pleasure came, it was with more power, slow and deep, gathering up the heart before the last sweeping plunge into darkness.

Elaine lay on her stomach, her body draped over a bolster. Graham nestled himself over her, her derriere pressed intimately to him. He rested his cheek against her smooth white back and decided he'd never felt so drained in his life.

Or so happy.

Never had he made a better decision than coming back to her. He was just damn grateful she hadn't slammed the door in his face. Truthfully, he wouldn't have faulted her if she had. He was still a little scared about getting her son to accept him, but he would work at it. Every day.

"I think we forgot more rules," she murmured.

He kissed her shoulder. "No kidding. Am I too heavy?"

She made a sound that sounded like a negative, then reassured him by taking his hand and pressing it to her side. He reached under her to cup her breast. It was as if it had been made for him. Another man had had the right to think so one time. Graham turned that thought away. He wasn't going to be jealous of a dead man. He was here now and Elaine was naked and cozy with him. That was all that mattered. He intended to keep her in bed for the entire weekend.

"What are three little things that make you smile?" he asked, wanting to know the little things about her . . . and needing time to regain himself. If he didn't intend to let her out of bed the whole weekend, he'd have to pace himself.

"Vanilla fudge ice cream, Hy-Lit, and cats sunning themselves on the windowsill."

He chuckled. "Hy-Lit? Wasn't he a radio announcer?"

"A disc jockey. Best one in the sixties in Philadelphia. He's still on the radio, you know, and still on one of the most popular stations. Maybe you ought to get him to do a radio commercial for your pizzas. He has definite name recognition here."

Graham thought about that. "That's not a bad idea. He'd draw the parents who listen to him, and that means more family business."

"I see another meeting at the ballpark with Ed."

"I get to see you whenever I do." He caressed her breast, loving the way she curled back into him as he obviously hit her pleasure point. A small television on a tabletop caught his eye. Even though he hated to ask, he did. After all, it was Saturday afternoon. "Are you missing a ball game right now?"

"They're on a trip again." He relaxed until she added, "The game will be on tonight."

"Why do I think I ought to be jealous of nine other guys?"

"Twenty-five other guys. That's the full roster."

"Gee, thanks," he muttered, seeing all those young studs in his mind's eye. Twenty-five of them. He decided to make sure she was thoroughly occupied when the young studs went into baseball battle later.

She lifted her head enough to eye him in amusement and, as if she'd heard his thoughts, said, "Now, what interest would twenty-five young studs have in someone like me?"

He pressed himself intimately against her, rubbing his thumb and forefinger around her nipple. "Because you're beautiful and you're naked."

"Have you had your eyes checked lately? Men your age usually need glasses."

He playfully tweaked her nipple, and she flinched away, laughing. "I'm not over the hill yet," he admonished. "But I think my biggest worry is that you're going to be hot for twenty-five young studs while stuck with the old wreck here."

She reached around and patted his bottom. "I'll take the old wreck anytime."

"Thanks. I think. Now, where were we?"

"Right here." She wiggled her bottom against him, taking his breath away. "By the way, where does your mother live?"

He blinked. "I think we've just had a major

mood kill here. My mother? At a time like this you ask about my *mother*!"

"Prude."

"Not me. I've read *Fear of Flying*. My mother lives in Delaware. South by the shore. I'll take you to meet her. She'll like you. If it seems like she does mostly because I'm actually with a woman, don't mind that. She thinks I'm trying to be the world's greatest bachelor."

"Are you?"

"Hell, no."

But the truth was, Graham admitted, he was no more ready for marriage than Elaine seemed to be. Everything was so fragile with her, he didn't want to think beyond just dealing with the burgeoning of their relationship. Once this was solid, then he could think more.

"We need to know a lot more things about each other than ice cream and DJs," she said after a moment. She'd obviously read his thoughts again. "Like if this is just sex or something more."

"Elaine, you and I are old enough to know the difference between just sex and something more. You know this is something more."

"I know."

He pushed back the hair from her cheek and kissed it. "I knew it would be like this. That's why I couldn't stay away."

"All this will change when Anthony comes back."

He caressed her breast and rubbed himself against her. "This won't."

She drew in a shuddering breath. "No, this won't."

"But I'm not going anywhere," he whispered in reassurance. "We'll work it out."

"I hope so." She turned around in his arms, nearly taking all his rational thought when her breasts pressed against her chest. Only the worried look in her eyes stopped him from ravishing her on the spot.

"It'll take time, but it'll be all right," he said, kissing her cheek.

He was making promises, maybe promises that he couldn't keep. He knew it, but he couldn't help himself. One thing he did know was that he would do his utmost to get her son to like him.

The rest of the weekend was spent, to his satisfaction, in Elaine's bed, even to the extent that the ball game was turned on but never watched. She was far too occupied with the pleasure the "old wreck" was giving her.

And nothing pleased him more.

Graham left about an hour before Anthony was due back Sunday afternoon, with a promise of dinner on Tuesday.

Elaine, feeling as if her whole body had been deliciously pommeled by an expert masseur, straightened away all traces of her visitor. She wasn't ready to have Anthony walk into an affair that his mother was having. Or her in-laws. That would be a slap in the face to them, one she had no intention of delivering.

Oh, Lord, she thought as she settled into a bubble bath. She'd nearly seduced Graham in the foyer before he'd left. Never had she had so much love-making before. She wished they'd had hours more to themselves before the world intruded. Hours and hours. She laid her head back against the cool porcelain and closed her eyes.

She was in deep with this man, and trying to control her spiraling emotions was impossible. Yet shutting the door on him yesterday would have been like slicing out her heart. She just wouldn't have been able to live if she had.

"Now the payment comes," she murmured.

A plaintive meow answered her.

She opened her eyes and stared at Mikey, who was standing in the doorway, staring at her. "I know. I have sinned."

The cat purred and walked toward her, as if happy she'd confessed. She closed her eyes and settled back, knowing he would brace his forepaws on the edge of the tub and sniff the bubbles. He followed true to form, but otherwise didn't disturb her.

Sometime later a noise downstairs brought her alert.

"Mom! We're here!"

"I'll be down in a moment," she called, scrambling to get out of her now-bracing bathwater. "I'm in the tub!"

When she went downstairs later, completely dressed and demure, she felt like a fraud as she kissed Joe's parents and gave Anthony a quick hug.

The world had intruded all too soon. Now it would begin.

EIGHT

Monday evening, just as Anthony was going up to bed, Elaine drew in a deep breath and said, "Anthony, I've arranged for you to be over at Steve's tomorrow night—"

Her son slewed around, staring at her.

She continued calmly, "I'm going out to dinner with Mr. Reed again."

The surprised silence froze over faster than Hell on vacation at the South Pole.

"You said you would try, remember?" she reminded him.

"But I thought . . . he acted all funny that time at the game," Anthony burst out. "And Aunt Cleo said that meant he was dumping you."

"Aunt Cleo says a lot of things just to be funny," Elaine told him, hoping she was handling this right. "But, yes, he was . . . unsure. We both were. We still are. But we . . . ah, had a long talk

this weekend, and we'd like to see each other
again."

"Mom!"

The sheer panic on her son's face broke her
heart.

"Anthony, honey," she said desperately, before
he could throw a fit. "Don't make this out to be
more than it is right now. None of us knows where
this is going, and I'm only taking it one day at a
time. That's all it is now. One day at a time. And so
should you."

He didn't say anything for so long, guilt flared
up in her like a sudden forest fire.

"Anthony . . ."

"Fine." He whirled away, out the front door.

Elaine sighed, wondering what else she could
do to reassure him that the threat he saw wasn't a
threat at all. She was trained to help kids like him
deal with exactly these kinds of family issues, yet
she felt she was failing miserably with her son. She
also wondered if she should have discussed the
weekend more with Anthony, maybe told him Graham had spent the night, but his reaction to a simple dinner killed that notion. She was being less
than honest, but he wasn't ready to hear it. If anyone who had noticed Graham's car had mentioned
it to Anthony, he would have brought it up. Probably he would have thrown it in her face. Maybe she
should cancel the dinner with Graham. . . .

Resentment flared up. Why couldn't she have a
little bit for herself? She wasn't being selfish to

want a private life. In trying to compensate for the missing parent, she had sacrificed a lot for Anthony, including long-denied needs. Now someone had come along, and no matter how tenuous the relationship, it was one she wanted to pursue. And the sooner Anthony got used to his mother having a private life, the better. *One day at a time*, she told herself firmly.

But the days stretched out deliciously endless, and she knew in her heart she was way past one day at a time. She couldn't stop herself either. Not from the moment she'd opened her front door to him . . . the first time.

When Anthony came in later, he didn't say a word, just stomped up to his room. Elaine sighed again and let him go. He needed time to deal with this, and so did she. Maybe she would ask Joan Harmon, the school counselor, about what she could be doing, even though her instincts told her she was already doing the right thing.

Elaine discovered that dinner with Graham was only a nice notion, however. She was halfway dressed for it the next day when he called.

"I have to cancel," he said abruptly. "Something's come up here that I have to handle myself. By the time it's done, it'll be too late for me to drive up from Delaware."

"Oh." Disappointment, sharp and bitter, was already wending its way through her heart.

"I'm sorry." His voice was softer. "This dinner

is important to us, and I hate having to cancel. How about tomorrow night?"

"There's a game," she said, staring at her unzipped back in the long door mirror.

"Can't you skip it?" The exasperation in his voice was heavy.

"The ladies are depending on me for their ride." She paused. "Besides, Anthony would throw a fit if we didn't go. The team's coming off a 6–1 road trip." She added, "Won six, lost one."

He groaned. "I can't go back to Ed again on such short notice to get his seats."

"They're playing a day game on Friday," she said helpfully. "A businessperson's special, so I'm free that night. Would you . . . would you want to change dinner until then?"

"Friday? Absolutely. I shouldn't have a crisis then, and to hell with it if I do. I'm truly sorry, Elaine."

"I understand," she reassured him.

"Are you really all right with this?"

"Yes."

A short time later she reluctantly hung up and sat down on her bed. It hurt, she thought, a bit surprised to realize she was. Even the change to Friday did little to ease her insecurity.

She called over to her neighbor, to alert Anthony she wasn't going anywhere after all. Her son was home within minutes.

"Mom!" he called out, coming up the stairs at a fast clip.

"I'm here," she replied, surprised he'd come home. She got to her feet and quickly finished zipping up her dress, even though she was going nowhere.

Anthony skidded to a halt just inside her bedroom. Mikey romped in after him, like a dog. "You're not going?"

"Mr. Reed had to cancel because he had an emergency at the office," she said, forcing a smile.

His face fell. "Oh."

Elaine had the oddest notion he'd been expecting her to have done the canceling. She felt as if she were a bone between two jealous dogs. Anthony was a little scared that he'd lose his mother, but he surely wasn't *jealous*.

Her son brightened. "That stinks, Mom."

"Oh, yeah," she agreed wryly. "But we're going out on Friday."

Anthony's eyes widened. "Oh."

"Steve's parents are going out that night, too, so she's arranging for a sitter for you and Steve."

"Oh." Her son's expression changed from bewilderment to determination. "He'll probably cancel again, the turkey."

"We'll see," she said noncommittally. She didn't have that much more confidence than her son.

"He will, you'll see."

Anthony left her with those damning words.

Elaine slumped down on the bed again, lying back this time. She covered her face with her arm, trying to ignore the lump forming in her throat. She put her emotions out on the line for this man, and she hoped her son was wrong about him.

Unfortunately, she couldn't shake the feeling that he was exactly right.

On Friday evening Graham pulled into Elaine's extra parking space fifty-five minutes late.

But he was there, he thought, getting out of the car, and considering the day he'd had, that counted for something. He picked up his apology bouquet. Even though he'd alerted Elaine he would be late, a dozen yellow roses wouldn't hurt.

Anthony was outside with some of his friends. The boys stood on the tiny front lawn, their faces cold masks. Graham felt like he was running a gauntlet.

"Hi, guys," he said, smiling bravely. The boys didn't answer, just watched him. He shifted the roses to his other hand and rang the doorbell. Elaine must have been standing right behind the door, waiting for his ring, because the door opened before he could even lower his arm.

"Hi," she said, smiling.

She looked terrific in a khaki dress that skimmed her generous curves. A big red plaid scarf, draped across one shoulder and knotted intricately, brought out the dark highlights in her hair. But the most intriguing part was the line of black buttons that marched down the front of the dress from throat to knees. He wanted to open every one of them.

Feeling the audience at his back, he held out the flowers. "I'm sorry I'm late."

She took the flowers from him and opened the door even wider. "They're beautiful. Thank you. Come in while I put them in water."

He walked into the house and shut the door gratefully behind him. "Tough crowd out there."

Her smiled drooped a little. "They're kids."

"I know. I even remember." He drew her into his embrace, not even caring that he'd crush the roses between them, and kissed her until her hips melted against his. When he raised his head, his breath was already harsh in his lungs. "Better get those flowers in water or we'll never get out of here."

She shuddered and opened her eyes. "I know."

Somehow they got to the kitchen without falling further into temptation. Graham wondered how he'd make it through what would be a platonic evening—or better described as hell on earth as far as he was concerned.

Elaine's fingers seemed to be all thumbs as she got out a plain glass vase and tried to cut the end of the rose stems. "Here." Graham took the roses out of her hands and stuck them in the vase. "You can cut them later."

She groaned, her face turning pink. "Elaine the klutz strikes again. Why didn't I think of that?"

He grinned. "I like Elaine the klutz. She makes me feel wanted and useful."

"You own your own company. How could you not feel wanted and useful?"

"Because it's not the same." He shoved the last rose in the vase, then turned to her. "I've missed you this week."

Her smile trembled. "I missed you too."

"If I kiss you now," he said, feeling heat wash through his body, "I'll disgrace myself and we'll never get out of here."

She nodded. "I know."

They managed to leave without giving in to their primitive urges. It was just as well they didn't, because the boys were still there, obviously waiting. Graham wondered if Anthony would have come in had they taken a long time to return. Probably. He remembered his reaction to his own mother's first date after his father had died. He'd no doubt been just as unpleasant. Even though he knew it wasn't him, that didn't make him feel better. Matters were worsened when Elaine told Anthony to behave for his sitter. Anthony looked incensed at the childish treatment, and Graham couldn't blame the kid. But the murderous look was then turned on him, as if the whole thing were his fault in the first place.

He'd have to do something to bring the boy around, for if he didn't . . .

The notion bothered him all through what should have been an intimate dinner at a swanky restaurant in Center City. Even though they talked about little things to get to know each other better, afterward he couldn't quite remember what she'd said. Then other thoughts crowded in, taking his mind elsewhere as they drove toward her town house.

"I don't want to take you home," he said honestly. The evening was ending far too soon, and he'd wasted most of it on something that he could have considered when he was away from her. Now he didn't want to consider it at all. He only wanted to consider her. He needed to cement their relationship more now, for it seemed even more tenuous in ways.

She turned to him, her face glowing in the dim interior lights. "I don't want to go home, either. I . . . last weekend was wonderful, but I feel like it opened doors that I can't close now."

He grinned, liking that he did that to her. "I think my doors have been stuck wide open ever since you walked into that men's room."

She gave a throaty laugh. "I do make an interesting first impression, don't I?"

He glanced over. "Very. You still do."

He reached across the console and took her hand. "Would you like to stop for coffee or something? Even though we just ate?"

She hesitated. "I'd float away, truthfully."

He asked the question he hated to ask. "Then do you want to go home?"

"No." She didn't hesitate on this one, and nothing pleased him more.

"Is there a place where we could park? Just to talk."

She made a funny noise. "I don't think I've heard that line since I was about sixteen."

"I told you you make me feel like a teenager. But I don't trust myself if we go back to your house. I would . . . well, let's just say Anthony would get a biology lesson he doesn't need right now."

"Anthony's spending the night with his friend."

Graham moaned and squeezed her hand tightly. "Lord, woman, don't tempt me. I'd have you in the bed so fast . . ."

"There is a place that's quiet," she began, "and safe. For us."

"Much as I hate to ask . . . where?"

"My school."

"School!" He burst into laughter.

"No one's ever there this time of night," she said. "It's on the way home, and we could park in the parking lot behind the buses . . . to talk safely and undisturbed."

He let go of her hand. "Just point the way and we're there."

Her school wasn't a big one, but was surrounded by a grove of trees on three sides of the property. The line of buses went well on toward the back edge of the parking lot, and he pulled the Mercedes into the slot by the far one. This was quiet and safe, he thought, half pleased and half disgusted. Too bad they only felt like teenagers, because if they really were . . . He put the thought from his mind. They were here for privacy *to talk*. Nothing more.

But once the car's engine was turned off, an awkward silence settled over them. Elaine sat on her side, just staring ahead. Graham glanced over at her, finally saying, "Are you okay with all of this?"

"Yes . . . no." She looked at him and tried a weak smile. "I don't know, Graham."

"I meant what I said last weekend. I want to try because I need to be with you. You . . . I can't explain it, but you do something to me that I need in my life right now."

"I know, but that's just it. The 'right now.' This is all so new to me, and you're so . . . out of my league."

He laughed. "Hardly. I think you're out of mine."

"Graham, please." She looked wounded as she said, "You own your own company, you're rich and sophisticated. I'm poor and a klutz. Even Cinderella's fairy godmother would walk away from this one."

"I'm hardly rich," he said. "Most of my assets are tied up with my company, and it's only been in recent years that I'm not making pizzas eighteen hours a day. That's hardly sophisticated. Cinderella's godmother would take one look at me and say, 'Forget it, sweetheart. He's hardly up to snuff.' "

"You're beyond my snuff. And then there's my son, the Doberman pinscher. Coping with someone else's children is a lot to ask of anyone, but especially a bachelor who doesn't have a lot of experience with kids."

"None," he corrected her.

"Worse yet." She sighed. "The 'right now' seems almost impossible."

He sighed too. "I don't know what I can say to reassure you."

"Maybe that's the whole point," she said. "Maybe I just have to take all this on faith. It's either going to be something or it's not. But I can't walk away from it. I know that now."

He moved closer, as much as the console would allow. "That's what we both have to do, have faith. You have no idea what it meant to me for you to let me in last Saturday. No idea."

She drew in a deep breath, her breasts swelling deliciously under her dress. "You have no idea what it meant to see you on my doorstep."

He took her hand and kissed it, loving the feel of her satiny skin and slender fingers against his mouth and tongue. "I need to be with you, Elaine."

Her voice wavered, as if desire were already taking hold of her. "I need to be with you, Graham."

He turned her hand over and ran his tongue

along the lines of her palm. She trembled as he murmured, "I missed you so much."

He squeezed her fingers, then stretched to kiss her, just under her ear. She curled into the kiss as his lips teased her soft flesh there. Her perfume, mingling with her own private scent, rose up through his senses. This was sheer torture, he thought, and he loved it. He hoped it didn't end.

She turned. Her hands came up and cupped his face, even as her mouth took his in a flame of sudden yearning neither of them could deny. He kissed her so fervently, he thought he would explode from it. His hand found her breast under the scarf, under the dress. He took the velvet weight in his palm, his thumb rubbing across the already pebbled nipple. The kiss went on endlessly until they made themselves crazy with the enforced restraint.

"I thought you said this was safe," he gasped out, burying his face in her neck. He began a trail of love bites, feeling as if he could feed off her flesh, so aroused was his need for her.

"Dangerous," she murmured, her fingers tugging at his hair almost in supplication for more. "You make me feel so dangerous."

"You make me feel like we've gone parking on a date. I'm all urges and all for you."

"Too bad we can't," she murmured. "Because, Lord, how I want to."

He paused and raised his head, his whole body almost convulsed with true knowledge and hopeful anticipation. "We're really not teenagers gone parking and so we couldn't . . . could we?"

She gazed back at him. "We're far too old to be behaving in such a scandalous manner."

He whispered something very scandalous in her ear.

"We shouldn't."

"We couldn't."

Her hands went to the buttons of her dress.

He pushed his seat back.

The lights were blinding.

"Omigod!" Elaine yelped, spotting the police roof lights behind the glare of the regular headlights. She tried to straighten and scramble back into her seat but she was wedged too tightly between Graham and the console.

Graham's hands stilled her. "It's okay. We're decent."

"Now."

"Be grateful he didn't come—"

She choked on his choice of words.

"—*arrive* ten minutes before. We'll be honest . . . somewhat honest with him, and hope we don't get a ticket. Just let me do the talking."

The fact that her dress was buttoned enough to disguise what they'd been doing didn't help her panic. She wrapped the open skirt around her bare legs. "Graham, this is *my* school. I can't get arrested here!"

He didn't answer. He was too busy rolling down the car window to speak to the policeman who had gotten out of his vehicle and was walking toward them. He directed his flashlight into the interior for one embarrassing second, then clicked it off.

"Ahem." The cop cleared his throat, but the situation got to him and he grinned knowingly. "I guess you weren't planning to vandalize the school, like the janitor thought."

Jim Tarbluth. Elaine hadn't realized the young custodian would still be there, or be that alert to spot an odd car in the parking lot. She swallowed back the lump of fear at how close she'd come to being exposed—in more ways than one.

Graham laughed. It actually sounded natural. "I know this looks . . . silly. But it's tough to find privacy for even a few moments when there are children at her house, and I live two hours away. I guess we didn't think."

The cop nodded knowingly. "I understand. My lady friend has two kids and we've had to resort to a strange thing or two for privacy. Well, just don't do it again . . . or find a better place. I don't want to have to write a report on this in the future."

"We won't," Graham promised.

"Thank you," Elaine whispered, turning her face in humiliation.

The policeman went back to his car and pulled out of the parking lot, taking it on faith that they'd leave. It was really nice of him, Elaine thought in relief.

Graham began to laugh. "Caught parking at our age."

Elaine moaned. "Only I would get caught at it by the cops."

"You're an exciting woman." He kissed her cheek.

She reared back. "That's what got us into trouble in the first place!"

He grinned wickedly. "Yeah."

"Oh, Lord! You like it." She scrambled over the console, ignoring the goring she received from the hand brake. She finally and primly buttoned up the skirt of her dress.

"Of course, I like it." He took her hand and brought it to his lips. "I've never met anyone like you. Straightforward and earthy."

"In other words, a dirty old woman."

He snorted in amusement. "Absolutely. You were terrific."

She smiled. She couldn't help it. Making love in a car had been forbidden . . . and exciting exactly for that reason. She was totally out of control with this man. He reached out and caressed her cheek. His hand was warm and strong, his fingers curving around her face in a beautiful fit that sent shivers down her spine.

"Elaine, just keep being the wonderful person you are."

She relaxed, then began to chuckle. "Oh, Lord, but you make me so bad."

"Do I? I like the sound of that." His fingers began to trail lower.

She took them and firmly set his hand on the steering wheel. "We better go home before our wonderfully conscientious custodian turns us in again."

By the time they arrived there, she discovered just how hard it was to let Graham leave, especially knowing that Anthony was at his friend's.

She was still awake an hour later when the phone rang. Even before she answered it, she knew who it was.

"You were speeding," she said by way of hello.

Graham laughed. "You knew it was me."

"It couldn't be anyone else after this night. What did you do? Tell a cop you had to get home to call a dirty old woman?"

"It works every time—especially when the cop has the hots for a dirty old woman too. It's a man thing."

"I guess so." She turned over on her side, her body sliding sensuously along the smooth sheets. Suddenly her lonely house and lonely bed were more than full. "I'm glad you couldn't wait to call this dirty old woman."

"This dirty old man can't wait to see his dirty old woman again. . . ."

They began to talk, and it was dawn before they finished.

NINE

The Phillies had won eight straight games and Graham had had eight straight dates with Elaine. Although they hadn't had to repeat their first parking venture, they had used quite a bit of ingenuity to make love.

It was his fault, Graham thought happily. He just couldn't keep his hands off her. And she responded. Boy, how she responded . . .

He settled into his seat next to Ed Tarksas at the Vet. He felt a little guilty at using Ed like this again, but he did have a tentative agreement with Ed's company to handle some advertising for Cove Pizzerias.

He hadn't told Elaine he'd be at the stadium that night, his first since that awful time when he'd broken off with her. Tonight would be a much better night, he thought with satisfaction. He felt as if he were making some kind of declaration by being there, and when he saw Elaine emerge from the concourse entrance, he felt it all the more.

She paused when she spotted him, then grinned broadly. He grinned back, his hands already itching to touch her. The three widows looked at him, then at her, eyebrows raised. Graham had a feeling Elaine hadn't said anything to them about their dates. Not that she needed to. Those three were extremely sharp ladies. Anthony, however, was looking anything but happy.

Graham's smile faded. No matter what he did, the boy was not coming around. Granted, they mostly saw each other when he picked Elaine up for dinner or a movie, but no easy greeting penetrated the boy's stonewall demeanor. Graham hoped that with time things would ease between them.

"Hi," he said, when they all piled into the seats behind him.

"Hi, honey," Cleo said, grinning widely. "And you too, honey," she added to Ed.

Ed grunted in reply.

"Girls, say hi to the suit men."

"Hello," Jean and Mary chorused. Their grins were even wider than Cleo's.

"You come to see us?" Cleo asked, patting Graham on the shoulder. "We're the sexiest women here, aren't we?"

"Absolutely," Graham agreed. "I have to hold Ed back."

The women burst into laughter. Even Ed cracked a smile.

Elaine leaned forward. She wasn't laughing. "I got my charge bill today and there seems to be a credit on it that doesn't belong there."

Graham chuckled, knowing what she was talking about. "No kidding?"

She eyed him, looking miffed. "No kidding. I assume you got Boyd's to give me a credit and you paid for the suit yourself."

"I couldn't let you pay for that," he said in his defense, bewildered that he suddenly had to defend common sense.

"She bought him a suit," Jean said to Cleo and Mary.

"*Rightttt,*" Cleo replied, drawing out the word. "That's about all he'll get from this sugar mama."

Mary's beads clicked.

"Before everyone jumps to conclusions, like I'm rich beyond my means," Elaine began hotly, "my dry cleaner friend messed up his suit, so I replaced it, since I bugged him so damn much about letting me get it cleaned for him."

The women nudged one another in gestures reminiscent of Monty Python's "Wink-wink, Nudge-nudge" skit. They weren't buying her explanation.

Anthony looked stricken.

Graham smiled at the boy to take the edge off. "Sometimes a guy's got to be a gentleman. It's a guy thing, isn't it?"

Anthony's wide-eyed expression turned into a frown. At least he had the kid thinking. That was a step forward.

Cleo, bless her heart, reinforced it. "Anthony, honey, you've definitely got to get with the guy program. You been hanging around with just us women far too long."

She reached across Elaine and patted the boy on the cheek. Elaine smiled at her son, who smiled back. "Yeah, I guess so," he said.

"You come and sit next to your sugar mama," Cleo said with delightful wickedness to Graham. "And I'll sit next to Mr. Suit here. I don't want to hold him back from nothing."

"Thanks," Graham said, laughing.

Ed choked on his protest. Graham patted his arm in sympathy. He figured this would cost him something in Ed's advertising campaign somewhere down the road. It would be worth it, though, just to see Ed cope with Cleo. He also figured Ed had finally realized what Graham's interest in the games was really all about.

Graham was a big man and Cleo was no Kate Moss, so the seat exchange was made a little precariously on the narrow concrete walkway between the rows. He helped Cleo step down onto the seat itself, then to the lower walkway. She dusted off the seat bottom before sitting down.

"If he's any good, I'll let you trade places with me later," Cleo said to Jean and Mary, who guffawed. Ed hunched lower in his seat. He was probably hoping Cleo's Mr. Excitement didn't come up to bat.

Graham settled into the seat next to Elaine, loving the enforced coziness of his thigh against hers. "Hi, sugar mama."

She moaned. "I'll never live this down."

Graham laughed, then grew serious. "You're not really mad at me for having the bill for the suit credited to me, are you?"

"Of course I am," she said, glaring at him. "But I never should have brought it up here. I wouldn't have, except I got the darn thing today, and I was so angry with you about it. Leave it to me to pick my spots."

Graham had an urge to remind her of some of her "spots," but Anthony was on the other side of her, listening intently.

"Anthony." He leaned around Elaine. Her breasts pressed against his arm, and he nearly forgot what he was going to say. The sudden rush of desire along his veins swept all common sense from his brain. He forced away the notion of taking Elaine right there, right then, and damn the consequences. "Anthony, you don't need to see your mother pay a fortune to teach you a lesson about taking responsibility for your actions, do you?"

Anthony was bewildered. "I guess not."

"And by my ensuring your mother doesn't needlessly pay for something she shouldn't have to in the first place, you've now learned a lesson on being a gentleman, right?"

"Does this mean Mom can afford to get me the latest *Double Dragon* tape for Super Nintendo?"

"Probably."

"Great lesson, Mr. Reed," Anthony said, grinning at him.

Everyone laughed. Except Elaine.

"Either way, I'm still paying," she said.

"That's what sugar mamas are for," Graham said, taking her hand.

He sat back to watch the game.

"What!"

Elaine listened in disbelief as the disciplinarian at Anthony's school repeated that her son had been caught cutting classes. She had just finished her last class of the day when she'd been told a call was in the main office for her.

Flushing with anger, she said, "I'll be right over."

She signed herself out early, quickly got what she needed from her classroom, and was over at Anthony's school in record time. Her son was sitting in the main office, looking glum. When he glanced up at her, however, his expression turned to hostility.

She knew whatever had caused this, she was the source.

Disciplinary action was in the form of an in-school suspension and points that would cost the boy an upcoming school camping trip. That hurt.

Anthony looked ready to cry, and Elaine knew he was hit hard. She decided that when she got him out to the car, she wouldn't say a word. Not until they got home and she was cooled off enough to deal with him.

The car door hadn't even closed, however, before she was asking, "Why?"

Anthony shrugged and stared out the window.

The lid on Elaine's anger burst. "Dammit, Anthony, why did you cut classes?"

"I don't know."

"That's unacceptable!" She wheeled the car out of the parking lot, the tires squealing on the asphalt. She didn't care. "You will give me a proper answer or you'll be lucky if you see the light of day before you're twenty-five!"

"We don't have a basement, Mom."

She nearly wrecked the car. "Don't smart-mouth me." Taking a deep breath, she tried to control herself before she went berserk. "Anthony, this isn't like you at all. What's the matter? Why did you cut school? Did you just want to see what it was like?"

He didn't answer.

She probed further. "Did Steven cut with you?"

She knew all of Anthony's friends, and she had no doubt they were guilty of little misdeeds, as all kids were. But they were good boys, trustworthy. Maybe her son was in with a crowd he shouldn't be and was trying to prove himself with them, a parent's worst nightmare.

"No," he answered. "Just me."

"So you cut by yourself. Are you mad at me for something? Because if you are, I'm not feeling nearly as punished as you are right now, okay? In fact, other than being angry with you, I feel damn good."

"Thanks to that Mr. Reed." The sarcasm in her son's voice was heavy.

"Ahh." She felt the lightbulb coming on, but still she was puzzled. "But you seemed to like him the other night."

She glanced over in time to see her son shrug again. He didn't want to admit he liked Graham, she thought, and wondered how she could help her son through this.

"Did you really buy him a suit?"

"I *replaced* his ruined suit," she corrected. "There's a world of difference. And I replaced it because it was my responsibility to do so. I had spilled soda on it, I talked him into allowing me to get it cleaned, it got messed up in the process. I felt I could do nothing else but replace the suit. It was very kind of him to take care of the bill, but while he was being a gentleman, what he did wasn't right. Not really."

"So you won't see him again—"

"No." She said it very gently. "I will see him again, if he asks me."

Anthony's sulky expression returned.

"Anthony, I think you want to like Graham, but you feel like you're betraying your dad when you do. You're not. Graham's not looking to take anyone's place, believe me. And I love you. I love you even more now, maybe because you need it the most today. But cutting school to get back at me only hurts you. You're missing your camping trip . . . and you're grounded for a month. Including Phillies games."

"Mom!" Tears did well up in her son's eyes and spill over this time.

She hardened her heart against them, knowing she had to show him that this behavior wouldn't be tolerated at all.

"Mom, please, isn't my missing the camping trip enough?" Anthony pleaded. "Not the Phils."

"They're on a road trip for half the month, so it won't be so bad, honey," she said, smiling sympathetically. "But the grounding does have to stand."

"But what about Aunt Cleo and Aunt Jean and Aunt Mary? They need us to get them to the game."

"I'll arrange for transportation for them," she said. Inwardly she sighed. The only innocent being punished was herself. Or maybe she was not so innocent. Anthony had more than once expressed his dislike of her having a relationship. Guilt assailed her. What did single parents do in this situation?

It was a question she was still asking herself later in the week, when she and Graham went out to dinner. A babysitter was with Anthony—part of his punishment was that he couldn't stay at Steven's house for the duration—and that was another blow to his adolescent pride.

"I don't know what to say to him to reassure him that none of this is a threat to my love for him," she told Graham.

Graham was quiet for a long moment, slowly twirling his wineglass.

She sensed immediately that he was uncomfortable with the conversation. She wondered if he felt threatened in some way . . . or didn't want to get further involved with what looked to be a major domestic problem. Pain slid through her, rather like a slow-motion descent of tiles off a roof. The awfulness of it couldn't be stopped.

"Well," she said, shrugging. "Anthony and I will work on it, I'm sure. We'll probably want to kill each other in the process, but we'll work on it."

Graham grinned finally, in what was clearly relief. But the moment left her with a very bad feeling. He might say he was ready to accept her child, but he couldn't mean it. Not now.

She was cooler to him after that. She couldn't help it. She was also grateful that the evening would be a short one since he had a meeting before eight the next morning. The last thing she felt like was making love, especially in some uninhibited way again.

"I want you and Anthony to come and meet my mother this Sunday," he said as he dropped her off.

She gaped at him. "Really?"

He smiled and took her into his arms. "I think it's time you did. Besides, she knows I'm seeing someone and she's making noises."

Elaine melted against him, all her misgivings gone in this new step he'd offered in their relationship. "I'd love to meet your mother. And Sunday's fine."

"I know. The Phils are on the road again." He groaned. "Now I'm wondering if it's such a good idea. You'll compare notes."

"That's the risk you have to take."

He kissed her, his mouth hot and demanding and regretful all at the same time. He would come around, she thought, doing her best to drive away the doubts she'd experienced at dinner. He would come around.

Lenore Reed turned out to be nothing like the tall, stately, imperial woman Elaine had been expecting. She was short and plump for one thing, with gray hair unrelieved by any bottle. And her smile was warm and merry.

"Welcome, welcome," she said, coming down the front walkway of her small cedar-shake house on Delaware's Indian Bay. The Atlantic Ocean was less than a mile away, and the early-summer air was heavy with humidity and salt. Neither seemed to affect Lenore.

She took Elaine's hand and fussed over Anthony. Anthony had been miserable in the back seat during the three-hour ride down, even though it was a short reprieve from his grounding. Now he looked positively put-upon by the world, despite Elaine's conversation about best behavior with him before they left. Elaine had no doubt he intended to pull the typical teenage trick of keeping to the letter of the agreement while letting everyone know how much he was suffering. She resisted the urge to kick him. Not that she ever had, but the temptation was definitely there.

"Come in, come in," Lenore said, smiling at her. "I've got plenty to eat. You must be hungry after your long trip."

Elaine smiled back as they walked into the house. "Actually it was a lovely drive down. You have a beautiful place here."

"I moved down here after my Frank died," Lenore told her in confidential tones. "It's lonely but I do love it. It wouldn't be so lonely if my son came around more often."

"Aw, Mom," Graham said, making a face.

Elaine grinned at him. The man had his own corporation, and his mother could still dispel the executive image with a few choice words.

"Well, you should come more often," Lenore admonished.

Graham gave Elaine a pointed look, as if to say she was the fault. Elaine just shook her head.

"Graham tells me you're a schoolteacher," Lenore began in a charming grilling, but a grilling

just the same, that continued through the small
feast Lenore called a snack.

Elaine found herself smiling with affection at
the older woman. Lenore would be a perfect fit for
the Widows' Club, she thought. But it was clear
through the nonstop chattering Lenore did that
Graham's mother was lonely. Elaine felt guilty for
the one dinner Graham had postponed with his
mother to be with her. She wondered how many
other dinners Lenore had had postponed since
Graham and she had been seeing each other.

Her own son picked his way through the meal,
the unhappy look on his face magnifying to full-out
uncooperation whenever Graham or Lenore ad-
dressed him—and especially when Elaine did. She
was about to take him into another room and give
him a firm talking-to when Lenore stepped in.

"I have some good fishing in my little cove out
back," Lenore said to Anthony. "Do you fish?"

Anthony shrugged.

"Well, then, come on and we'll set you up with
a rod and some bait."

Elaine grinned in amusement as Anthony was
hustled by this grandmotherly steamroller toward a
small dock behind the house. The bay curved into a
beautiful cove, just right for fishing.

"Did you name your pizzeria chain after this?"
Elaine asked Graham.

He laughed but shook his head. "No—"

"Heavens no," Lenore broke in as she loaded
Anthony's arms with all sorts of fishing gear. "I

bought this place five years ago. I thought it was kismet the first time I saw it."

A few minutes later Lenore, a hat on her head, was sitting on a camp stool while Anthony made his seat directly on the grayish boards of the dock. He had his pole in hand and listened intently as Lenore gave him a fishing lecture and charmed him into smiling and laughing with her.

"She's a jewel," Elaine said as she and Graham settled into some lawn chairs on the deck up at the house.

He grinned. "I thought you'd like her."

"I think Anthony does too."

"All my friends liked her when I was Anthony's age."

She turned to him, surprised at the deprecating tone in his voice. "You sound as if that was a bad thing."

"No." He smiled. "It's just a little disheartening to see her make headway so easily, even though I know she's not a threat and he sees me as one."

His words sent a shaft of fear into her stomach. Just as she had the other night, she felt that sense of doom. And if Graham was beginning to feel that way, then he *would* doom their relationship. Usually a person's enthusiasm could carry him through the impossible, while the lack of it would ensure failure.

"Maybe," Graham said, "I ought to take some lessons from my mother on how to handle kids. After all, she still handles me pretty well."

"She does it very well." Elaine smiled and took his hand. Inside she fiercely chased out any last nagging thoughts. She cared so much about this man, and now he was letting her into the closest part of his life. She wouldn't waste any more doubts on insecurities.

Anthony caught two blues, small ones that had wandered into the bay. He was ecstatic even though they threw them back, but the fishing had worked. Her son was more cheerful and, when he wasn't paying attention, was actually having a good time.

The cap of the day came when they went out for dinner—on the boardwalk in Rehoboth Beach at a Cove Pizzeria.

"You're kidding!" Elaine exclaimed, laughing, when Graham ushered them under the awning and into the wide entryway.

"Never," he said, grinning delightedly for having fooled her into thinking he was taking them to another place to eat. Business was busy, even though it was a Sunday evening, but despite the traffic the place was nearly pristine. The view of the ocean and beach was spectacular, since they were practically smack on both. Graham had a gold mine in this one alone, Elaine thought, and she wondered about the rest of the chain.

Graham called to the man behind the counter. "Lou! Need another pizza tosser tonight?"

"Always when it's you, boss!" Lou came around the counter, his hand outstretched. He was in his fifties, obviously the manager of this particular pizzeria, and familiar with Graham and his mother, for he bussed Lenore's cheek.

"This ought to be something," Elaine whispered to Anthony as Graham rolled up his sleeves in clear preparation to cook.

"Anthony, come and help me make a real man's pizza," Graham said, taking them both by surprise. "We'll put anchovies on your mother's."

Elaine and Lenore immediately nudged the boy forward, who didn't go reluctantly for once. Evidently he liked the idea of revenge by little smelly fishies.

Elaine sat with Lenore at a booth, but her focus was on watching Graham and Anthony together. The man talked easily to the boy, giving direction and advice . . . and most of all laughing with her son.

He had taken a page from his mother's book and was charming Anthony.

Maybe there was hope after all.

TEN

I love you.

The words rang in Elaine's head as she convulsed in ecstasy under Graham's driving body. He cried out something unintelligible, then buried himself one last time into her, his seed pulsing through her soft depths. The pleasure was better each time she was with him.

She surfaced to find tears leaking down past her temples, the release emotional as well as physical. Graham's weight was heavy on her, but she found contentment in his flesh pressed to hers.

He raised his head. "You're crying. What's wrong?"

"Nothing." She sobbed and brushed at the tears with the back of her hand. "It was so good."

He smiled wryly. "I'm glad you think so."

Truly she wasn't crying because she hadn't said

I love you out loud. She wasn't ready to. And he hadn't said it first.

Another sob escaped her.

"Did something else happen with Anthony?" Graham asked suspiciously.

"No. Oh, no."

"He seems more congenial now about my seeing you."

She nodded. "Especially as school's out. He likes staying overnight at Steven's, so you know he's happy about tonight. And I'm staying overnight at your place, so I'm happy too."

"You sure?" He looked worried.

"Yes, I'm sure. We just have to get me home before he realizes I've been away all night."

Graham chuckled. "I've set the alarm, although I don't intend to let you sleep at all."

"I would hope not." She kissed his shoulder. Things had been better between him and Anthony since their visit to his mother's a couple of weeks earlier. Not much better, but better. Still, she wasn't going to risk such an open declaration to her son yet.

She realized the moment of intimacy was slipping away. She rubbed her hands down Graham's back, trying to regain the sense of isolation in his bedroom. But she could tell his mind was already past their lovemaking.

A few moments later he rolled off her. She told herself it was because he felt he was growing heavy, but she sensed the emotional withdrawal in him.

And in her. She didn't know how to stop it. Their relationship wasn't just sex, but it wasn't much more than that either. An invisible wall seemed to be growing higher and higher between them. How would they break through when she was as insecure as he? The Phillies were in a bad losing streak right now, having dumped their last five games. Maybe she and Graham were in a losing streak too. Maybe they wouldn't come out of it.

She told herself she was imagining things. Everything was still so new between her and Graham. Anthony *was* more congenial. She'd met Graham's mother. Besides, how ready was she for deepening the commitment? Not ready, she admitted. She couldn't expect more from him than she could give. That wouldn't be fair. They were moving along nicely, everything in its own time.

So why did she hurt so much because she couldn't say "I love you"?

The call came after midnight.

Graham reached out, encountered warm flesh between him and the nightstand telephone. Disoriented with sleep, he had a moment of surprise, then realized it was Elaine in his bed. He smiled sleepily and reached across her to pick up the phone. She came awake with a start.

"Hello?" he said.

"Graham." It was one of his vice presidents. "We were hit with two robberies tonight."

Graham jackknifed into a sitting position. "What!"

"What?" Elaine gasped, sitting up with him. "What? What?"

"Two of my places were robbed," he said to her.

She visibly relaxed. The darkness couldn't hide it. Graham realized she was thinking of her son. Unfortunately, it was his "kids" that were in trouble. Putting her arm around his shoulders, she turned her attention to his problems.

"Where?" he asked into the phone.

"The one in Dover and the one in Clayton. The police say they're pretty sure the incidents were just coincidental. The manager in Clayton was shot."

Elaine gasped, having overheard the news.

Graham's stomach crawled. "How bad?"

"He's in Christianna Hospital in critical condition. They've probably started the surgery by now."

Graham was already pushing the covers back to get out of bed. Christianna was just up the road from his condo. "Cover his bills for whatever our insurance plan doesn't cover. I'm going over there. Does he have family?"

"A wife and two young ones."

Graham sucked in his breath. "Okay, take care of whatever they need."

He hung up and turned to Elaine. "I have to go."

She turned on the light, blinking at its brightness. Even in his state, he noted she made a beautiful sensual picture with her hair disheveled and one hand holding the paisley coverlet against her creamy breasts. No wonder she made him crazy.

"I'll come with you," she said.

"No. There's no reason for you to go." He went to his dresser to get clothes. "There's nothing you can do, anyway. There's nothing I can do, but it's my responsibility. The man works for me."

She ignored his further protests and got dressed. He gave up trying to persuade her to stay home and admitted he was grateful for her presence.

The hospital was a zoo of people running around in organized chaos. He felt incredibly guilty when he faced the scared young wife of his Clayton manager who was in surgery. Elaine took her under her wing, seeming to know exactly what to say to this woman whose life might be shattered. He wondered how much of this she had lived through when her husband had died, then realized it must have been almost exactly the same.

Elaine called Anthony. They had planned to have her home before morning, but that wouldn't happen now. He heard her reassure her son that she was fine and would be home by evening. Graham felt left out somehow in the communication process, as if he should have been important to the reassurance chain. As he listened to her, he realized her focus would always be on Anthony first. He supposed he understood it as a part of parenting, but he was beginning to wonder if he really could compete with it.

They stayed until the surgery was done and the patient was out of recovery and in his room. The doctor had assured them the surgery was a complete success. Graham saw to the wife's immediate needs, then finally he and Elaine went home.

Inside his condo he saw the sterility in which he lived. Expensive furniture with not a sculpture piece out of place nor a pillow touched since it had been plumped by the cleaning service. No magazines were left lying half open on the coffee table, no pet even to create some domestic warmth. No life.

Nothing, except Elaine. He realized what a brilliant burst of color she brought into his existence.

He took her in his arms. She leaned against him, her hands stroking his shoulders in comfort.

"I need this," he whispered, holding her tightly to him.

"So do I," she said, her fingers threading into his hair.

He kissed her, his tongue swirling gently with hers. Nothing made him feel more alive than the honeyed sweetness of her mouth. His hands roamed her body. He wanted to feel all the complexities that made her what she was. He wanted her. The urgings were already coursing through his body, refusing to be denied. Coming from tragedy, he wanted to renew himself in the most basic act of life.

Her hands gently pushed his away, and she lifted her head. "I have to go."

He blinked, disoriented. "What?"

She nodded. "I really have to go. I have to get home to Anthony. He's upset. I could hear it through the telephone."

Graham's heart dropped. He didn't know how to fight a child's needs—he knew he couldn't—but he couldn't help feeling neglected too.

A funny look came into her eyes at his hesitation. "I have a son, Graham. I can't neglect him."

"I never said you should." He realized how defensive he sounded. He calmed himself. "Of course you shouldn't. I'll take you home."

"Why don't you stay for dinner?" she suggested, smiling as if to take the sting from the moment.

He had a feeling Anthony wouldn't be a willing partner to the suggestion, not when he put himself in the kid's shoes. If he were thirteen and feeling neglected, he certainly wouldn't want the cause foisted on him. Besides, Elaine would have enough to cope with, what with Anthony now knowing she'd spent the night with a man. The boy might have had suspicions before, but now he had positive confirmation.

Graham shook his head. "I better get back to the office right away. I should be there now."

"Oh. Of course. I could try and get someone to pick me up—"

"No." He nudged her away from him so she could get her things. "I want to take you home first. It's important for me to do that."

"Then come for dinner Saturday night," she said. "We don't have a game to go to because the Phillies are on the road again."

"I get the crumbs again because the studs are out of town," he complained.

"How true."

"I'll take it. But only if you make one of those salad things."

She chuckled. "What else did you think you were getting? Chateaubriand and Moët?"

He nuzzled her neck. "That's for your next visit here. Only I pour the champagne all over your naked body and lick it off."

Her breath caught. "Ooohhh, wicked . . . very wicked. What time should I be here?"

On the way back to her place Graham spent most of the drive on the car phone, talking with his office. Elaine did kiss him good-bye, but he barely noticed; at that point he was too involved in the business of the crisis aftermath.

It wasn't until he was halfway back down the interstate that he realized he'd never even waved to Anthony, who had been playing basketball at the street hoop in front of his friend's house.

He'd catch the boy next time.

—◆————————————◆—

"I thought you said he'd be here at seven."

Elaine set aside her own internal worries to re-assure her son. "It's only seven-thirty. I'm sure he's delayed in traffic or something, Anthony."

Her son looked dubious. She couldn't blame him. Her own stomach was churning with anxiety. What kind of traffic could Graham be involved in on a Saturday night? It wasn't a work day, and shore traffic was Friday and Sunday nights, so that wasn't the problem.

His lateness was all too reminiscent of another man's lateness one horrible night. At least it was for her. She looked out the window several more times, then went to the telephone to call Graham's home and office.

Anthony was at her side by the time she fruit-lessly hung up. She forced herself to smile. "No answer. That means he's on his way." Knowing what was probably preying on her son's mind, she added, "This isn't like your father—"

"*He's* not my father and you can't make him that!"

"I wasn't saying he is, and I'm not trying to," she replied as calmly as possible. Anthony had not said a word about her staying overnight at Graham's, though their plans to be circumspect had been lost in the robbery disasters. Her son had expressed his feelings on the subject, however, in sarcasm and rebellion. "But we can't help remembering that because Graham's late for dinner, can we? And that's all he is . . . just late for dinner. And it'll be the last time he'll be late for dinner, because I'll kill him when he finally does get here."

Anthony smiled. "Fine by me."

Unfortunately, she had a feeling her son meant it. Why was it every time she thought things were getting better, she discovered they weren't? Not even close, she thought while watching her son walk back into the living room.

And where the hell was Graham, and why *hadn't* he called? Panic shot through her, her hands trembling in response. Eventually she fed her son, who didn't eat that much, a telltale sign of trouble from a growing thirteen-year-old. She didn't bother to eat at all. She couldn't. Not until Graham arrived or she heard from him.

When he finally did show up, he was almost two hours late. She rushed outside, far more furious than relieved at the sight of him.

"Where the hell have you been?" she demanded.

"Working," he said, backing away from her as if recognizing he'd done something terrible.

"Why didn't you call?" She could feel the tears pushing at her throat and swallowed them back. "Why didn't you call?"

"My car phone is on the blitz. I didn't know it until I tried to use it to call you about being late." He looked at her closely. "I'm sorry, Elaine. I didn't realize my not calling would upset you so much."

"It's just that it reminded me—"

He uttered a barnyard curse. "I never even thought of that." He put his arms around her. "Lord, I'm sorry. I'll stop and call next time."

"Okay." Her anger vanished as she felt his body comfortingly against her own.

He let her go and they walked to the house together. Anthony was standing at the front door.

"You're late," he accused.

Elaine's stomach clenched at the animosity emanating from her son. She knew he had to have been reliving some terrible moments, but Graham didn't deserve to bear the brunt of the child's anger and grief.

"I'm sorry," Graham said, not at all defensive. He smiled at the boy. "I didn't mean to put a scare into you and your mother."

"I wasn't scared, but you weren't fair to Mom to make her worry."

"You're right. I wasn't. But it will never happen again."

"I'm sure Graham was tied up over those robberies," Elaine said, opening the door and backing her son into the foyer. "We can cut him some slack. *This time.*"

"I'm so grateful," Graham said, grinning at her. He walked inside. "I'm starved. Do I still get dinner?"

"I'll heat it up."

"Heat?" He frowned. "I thought I was getting one of your salad things."

"I actually cooked, all the more to make you feel guilty, my dear."

Graham looked at Anthony. "I really am in trouble, aren't I?"

The boy didn't answer.

She couldn't leave Anthony and Graham alone in the living room, a perfect setup for a child hell-bent on punishing an adult. She decided to defuse the situation before it started. "Anthony, it's not dark out yet, so why don't you take Graham out to shoot some baskets while I get dinner going. I remember he once said he was a basketball man."

Anthony didn't say anything for a moment, then nodded and went to get his basketball from his room. Graham took the opportunity to pull her into his embrace and kiss her. Like lightning, sensuality ripped through her. She clung to him, wanting him so much and knowing they would not make love that night.

The sound of oversized feet in oversized high-tops clumping down the staircase brought them back to their senses. They broke apart just before Anthony came into view bouncing his basketball on the freshly washed tiles.

"Don't bounce the basketball in the house," Elaine said automatically.

Anthony grunted a reply, the basketball still being bounced, as usual, as her son walked out of the house.

"They listen so well, don't you think?" she asked in general.

"It's what kids live for." Graham stripped off his jacket and tie, then rolled up his sleeves. "I know what you're doing, sneaky woman, but I haven't played hoops for years. Call an ambulance when I collapse."

"Just collapse *after* dinner or I'll really be ticked."

He chuckled and went out the front door, assuredly girding his basketball loins for the challenge. Elaine went into the kitchen to reheat her roast. She took the opportunity to watch man and boy discreetly from her open kitchen window, grateful that it was cool enough to keep the air-conditioning off. She might be able to hear what they were saying.

Anthony had the ball and was trying to get past Graham's waving hands. When he couldn't get a shot off to the basket, Graham stopped and showed the boy how to fake out the guard to get past him. Several more instructions were given on several other points of shooting and blocking. Some of Anthony's friends gathered, and eventually a little game was initiated.

Fascinating, Elaine thought, as her son grinned and laughed, he and Graham teamed up against four other boys. It was like some kind of tribal ritual being passed down, but more important, this was what Anthony had been missing. A man with whom to share his experiences and commonality.

The actual instruction in pizza making or basket-ball didn't matter. Only the male bonding did. And Graham . . . he'd gone along amenably with Anthony that night. Still, she wished she felt more secure about his commitment to their relationship. She wished . . .

"If wishes were horses, then beggars would ride," she murmured. She could wish a lot of things, but whatever would be, would be.

Still, there was promise tonight. Maybe what would be, would be good.

Anthony had long gone up to bed, and Graham settled back on the sofa, his arm around Elaine as they watched the late news together. He didn't want to leave, he thought. He didn't want to watch the news either.

He lifted Elaine's hair away from her nape and kissed the sensitive skin there, liking the way she shivered in response. "Dinner was great," he said. "Dessert's even better."

She chuckled. "Don't start something you can't stop."

"I wasn't planning to."

She leaned away from him, looking solemn. "Graham, Anthony could come downstairs at any time."

"You worry too much."

"Maybe. But he's on the fence now, and I don't want to push him off."

"I think you're being overprotective, Elaine. Anthony was fine when we played basketball. Damn near killed me, but he was great. And we had a nice chat at my mother's the other week. I'm making progress."

"Maybe, but parenting is more than nice chats. And I don't think you have a notion of what overprotective is. Anthony's coping with a big change in his life right now. If I want to give him time to accept you, accept us, then I would think you'd understand that."

"I don't want to fight with you," he said. It had been a bad week, and he didn't want to cap it off with a worse weekend. "I do understand, but I also think we ought to let nature take its course."

"Graham, we've only been seeing each other for a couple of months. We don't even know where this is going."

"All I wanted was a kiss," he complained.

She grinned reluctantly. "We know perfectly well what you wanted."

"Okay, so I'm a sex fiend where you're concerned." He drew her closer. "I want you, Elaine. I've missed you and I want to be with you."

She ran her hands across his shoulders. "And I've missed you. But we have to have a little restraint."

He traced her breast with his finger, then took the full curve in his hand, rubbing his palm across the rising nipple. Elaine's eyes fluttered down and her breathing grew heavy.

"A little restraint," he said hoarsely. "A very little."

Maybe Graham was right, Elaine thought, watching her son whoop loudly as one of his favorite players, John Kruk, slammed a monster homer into the Phillies bullpen. Maybe she was being overly protective of Anthony. But he'd been through so much already, more than most children should ever have to go through. She didn't want to see him hurt again.

Still, he *was* better with Graham. And Graham *was* better with him. Maybe she needed to stop looking for holes where there weren't any.

Anthony turned to her with a big grin on his face. "Awesome, Mom."

She grinned back. "They're lookin' good again. But you look better."

"Of course I do. School's out."

She laughed. "I know *exactly* how you feel."

She did feel good that night. The seats in front of her were empty. She'd known Graham wouldn't be there because he was working late. She didn't mind, although he had muttered something about the "studs" she'd be with. She watched Phillies catcher Darren Daulton take his long, lanky strides to the plate. Even from the 300 level, the man still looked terrific. Maybe Graham did have a point, she thought, objectively admiring the back view the baseball gods had presented her with.

"Mmm-mmm, now that's sugar in a sweet package," Cleo said.

"I'll say," Mary chimed in, her beads clacking.

"I wouldn't throw him out of my bed, but he better hit the damn ball out of the park," Jean said, being ever practical, although the Vet was a completely enclosed stadium. "Out of the park" meant into the upper deck, about as out of the park as a ball could get. "We're still behind by two runs, and it's the seventh inning."

Elaine looked over at her son. Anthony was just staring at the batter intently, his thoughts no doubt on baseball and oblivious to anything else.

"Look at Elaine, girls. She's so in love with her guy that she can't see Darren for Mr. Suit."

Elaine turned sharply to Cleo. Even Anthony came out of his reverie enough to turn red in the face. Elaine said, "I'm only *seeing* Graham. Don't make more out of it than it is."

"Uh-huh," the three said in a fair imitation of the Pepsi Girls.

"Your Mr. Suit's got a sweet package too."

"But can he hit the ball out of the park?"

"Look at her face. I'd say a homer every time."

"You three are dirty old ladies," Elaine said. "And you ought to be ashamed of yourselves, especially in front of Anthony."

"Honey, life's too short for shame," Cleo said. "And don't you worry about Anthony. He's a big boy now. You just have your fun and be happy. And we'll keep teasing you about it."

At that moment, Daulton's bat connected with a slider that had hung up over the heart of the plate. The ball went sailing over the wall in left center field.

"Out of the park," Jean said.

"Oh my, yes, out of the park," Mary said.

"*Way* out of the park," Cleo added.

Elaine sat back in her seat and thought about her own "sweet package." Most definitely out of the park.

ELEVEN

"He's not at Steve's or any of his other friends'!"

Graham felt the sucker punch deep in his stomach. His private line had rung in the midst of his conference with his two vice presidents. Elaine had been on the other end. Anthony, it seemed, couldn't be found.

"Are you sure?" he asked. The two vice presidents stared curiously at him.

"Of course I'm sure," Elaine said. "He knows we have to leave for the game at five. He's always home long before then. When he didn't come home at the time he was supposed to, I started calling. What do you think I did? Stood on my head and twiddled my fingers?"

The anger in her voice was palpable. He realized he had sounded as if he didn't believe her. The question was incredibly stupid. And that was how he felt. Stupid.

"I'm sorry," he said. "I only meant . . . it was just one of those dumb, automatic responses."

"I know." Her voice got shaky. "Graham, he'd never miss a game. Something's happened! I know it."

First him and now Anthony bringing back bad memories for her. Anthony ought to know better, though. Where the hell was the kid anyway? She was right; he wouldn't miss a game.

Graham knew he had to be calm for her. Instinct told him this was a case of teenage neglect and nothing more. Anthony had probably forgotten the time and was just late. After all, the boy was thirteen. "I'm sure he's fine, just late getting back from wherever he is. Probably he met up with another friend from school, someone he usually doesn't hang with, and went to his house and forgot to call. And forgot the time. Or they went to a mall or a movie with the other kid's family and they're not back yet. He's a teenager and they'd forget their heads if they weren't screwed on tight. At least that's what my mother said whenever I did something dumb like this. Why don't you call back some of his regular friends and see who else he was friendly with from school? Then check with them. Call me back and keep me posted."

"You're not coming?"

Graham frowned. There was no reason to drop everything . . . yet. He hoped there wouldn't be a reason. Besides, by the time he got there, Anthony would be home already. "Elaine, he's just late." He glanced at the clock on his desk. "A little more than an hour late. Logic tells me he's only neglectful—"

"Neglectful! Do you know how many kids are snatched? By the time we figure out he's not being neglectful, he'll be six states away and untraceable!"

He forced himself to stay calm. She was very upset and overreacting. "Elaine, Anthony's only late. I guarantee it. If you call out the riot squad now, he'll never forgive you the humiliation. Give the boy a chance to come home, but in the meantime call any kid he could have possibly come into contact with from school."

"I can't believe you're not coming. I need you. I need you now."

"Elaine, be sensible about this—"

"Sensible! I'm a parent. But I'm forgetting . . . you're not."

The words knifed deep. His expression must have been telling, because his two vice presidents suddenly found the ceiling infinitely more interesting to look at.

"No," he said, "I'm not. But I am trying to help you as best I can right now. Elaine, please get back on the telephone and call every kid anyone can think of to track him down, okay?"

"Fine." The bang on the other end of the line indicated her reaction to his advice. But she'd do it. He knew that.

He hung up his own receiver more quietly. The

moment he did, every bone in his body screamed for him to get up and go to her. Panic, he thought. He'd advocated giving the boy a chance to come home. Chances were, he'd no sooner dismiss the meeting to go there than Anthony would show up. He took a deep breath. "Where were we on those projected revenues for the next five years?"

Fifteen minutes later Graham realized he hadn't listened to a single thing either of the other men had said. His whole attention was focused on the crisis an hour away. Anthony hadn't come home and Elaine was in distress. Suddenly they were *his* family, and they could be in real trouble. He dismissed the meeting, knowing he was no good for this right now. After the men left, he began to pace his office, his mind racing way ahead to all kinds of tragedies.

He called Elaine and knew the minute her anxious "Hello!" came over the line that Anthony wasn't home yet. "He's not there yet, is he?"

"What do you care?"

"I care very much, dammit!" he snapped, exasperated with her. "And you know it. Have you got some other kids' numbers?"

"Yes, yes. I'm on the phone with one now. Nobody's seen him."

"Okay. Keep trying. If he isn't home within a half hour, I'm coming up."

"Thank you." Her voice was low, contrite. "I'm sorry. I'm just worried."

"I know, sweetheart. But he'll be home and late

. . . and probably complaining that you're treating him like a baby."

"Lord, I hope so."

But Anthony wasn't. Graham was in his car in a flash, heading for the bridge to Jersey and damn all speeding tickets. He called several times from his car phone, but the boy still hadn't arrived home.

He pulled into the town house parking lot with a screech of tires. Elaine was already out the door and running toward him. He took her in his arms and she sagged against him, crying. He realized that this was exactly how it must have been the night of her husband's death. Now her son was missing. He felt awful for trying earlier to inject some calmness into her panic. It seemed now that they were way beyond calmness anyway.

"I called everywhere," she sobbed.

"I know. I'm sorry I was a jerk about this. We'll find him. I promise."

She only cried harder.

The faint ring of the telephone inside the house had her tearing out of his embrace. He followed her into the house. She was already on the kitchen phone. From the conversation, he knew she was talking to the police. His heart lifted and sank at the same moment. Either the news could be very good or very terrible.

When she got off the phone finally, she turned to him. Her face was red from crying and her cheeks tearstained. But there were no fresh tears. He took it as a good sign.

"He's safe. He's okay," she said, and her eyes watered again. "But the police picked him up on Route 30. He was hitchhiking."

"Is he crazy?" Graham blurted out, shocked. "What the hell was he doing hitchhiking?"

"He wouldn't tell the cops. I have to go get him."

"I'll drive you."

She nodded. "Thanks. I don't think I could drive myself. I can't believe it. Oh, Graham."

He wrapped his arms around her, and she had a good cry. Of relief this time. He kissed the crown of her head and stroked her hair back from her face, murmuring words of comfort. Finally she lifted her head. He kissed her mouth lightly. "I love you. Everything will be okay."

"That's the first time you've said that to me."

"That everything would be okay?"

"No, that you love me."

"It couldn't be," he said, positive it wasn't.

"Yes, it is."

"Then I should have been saying it ages ago, because I've always loved you."

"I love you." She shuddered and tightened her arms around him for a moment longer, then released him. "We have to go now."

He nodded.

They left together to get Anthony.

❧————————❧

At the police station Elaine wrapped her arms around her son, grateful that he was alive and whole. When she let him go, she said, "What were you doing, Anthony? Do you know how much you scared me and Graham?"

"Sorry," he muttered, volunteering nothing further.

She couldn't tell whether he was sullen or scared and decided it was fear first, then embarrassment, that he was trying to hide with an overlay of bravado. A bulging backpack sat on the floor next to his chair. She would wait until they were in the car to question him further.

"Let's get you out of here," Graham said, taking charge.

She was grateful for his presence. She truly was . . . now that he was there. But she couldn't forget his refusal to come to her when she first called, especially as she had been right all along about Anthony being missing. And she couldn't forget she had been there for Graham's crisis that day.

He *had* said he loved her, though. She'd needed to hear that so badly. This was not the time to sort out the confusion, she thought.

She was given a ticket for her son's hitchhiking and a warning about the dangers for children on the roadways. Her gratitude to The Above for her son's health changed to a growing anger at her son's dumb actions, for Anthony knew better. Way better.

When they were in the car, she turned to the

back seat, where her son was ensconced. "Now, just what the hell were you doing hitchhiking?"

Anthony shrugged in answer.

"Dammit!" she exploded. "You answer me, young man. You know I depend on you to behave, especially since your father died—"

"I was running away, okay?"

Shocked, she collapsed back in her seat. Running away! She'd seen the backpack, but hadn't given any thought to what it meant. In all the panic before, she'd never considered checking his room to see if anything was missing. "Running away! Anthony! Why?"

Her son's gaze shifted to Graham, then back to the floor. He shrugged. "I dunno."

"You don't know!" But suddenly she knew. He hadn't liked her growing relationship with Graham, and he'd expressed himself in a dangerous, attention-getting way.

"Maybe this is something better left for a cooling-off period," Graham said. His voice was calm, almost too calm.

"Cooling off!" She stopped herself, for if she continued she wouldn't be responsible for her actions. "Fine. You're grounded for a month, Anthony. Now I'm cooled off."

"That wasn't what I had in mind," Graham murmured.

She considered eviscerating him, then let the notion go. He wasn't a part of this, not really, and he was making it clear yet again that he was uncomfortable dealing with children problems. She couldn't blame him, she admitted. He was seeing the worst of it.

At home she wrapped her arms around her waist, feeling half sick, as she watched her son go up the stairs to his room.

Graham sighed.

"Welcome to the real world of family life," she said, her voice breaking.

"Hey." He smiled and rubbed her arms. "Hey, I've been there . . ."

She thought he was saying that he had once run away from home because his mother had been dating.

". . . I was a teenager once and had arguments with my mother, too, although I never ran away."

He might not have meant it as an indictment, but she couldn't help taking it that way. "I feel like the most rotten mother in the world."

"No, you're not."

She started to cry again. "Yes, I am. What a mess. I'm so sorry, Graham."

He pulled her to him. "You don't have anything to be sorry about."

He was infinitely patient and absolutely wonderful, and she loved him.

That was why the doom she felt hurt all the more.

❖━━━━━❖

It took a while and a long discussion late into the night, after Graham had left, but Anthony finally confessed his reasons for running away.

He lay in his bed, under the covers, looking young and vulnerable again. Mikey was curled against the boy's hip, sleeping. Anthony ran his fingers through Mikey's fur, the caress seeming as soothing to the boy as to the cat. But just as she suspected, it was her relationship with Graham that had motivated his act of rebellion.

Basically her son hated it.

"I know what you've been doing with him," Anthony said in a hurt voice. "I know he was here when I was at Grandmom and Grandpa's. Steve told me his car was here that night and then in the morning. I know you were . . . you were doing *it*."

She was sitting on the edge of his bed, yet felt like she was falling off it at the unexpected attack. Gathering her wits, she said, "We talked before, Anthony, about needs, adult needs. I . . . care about Graham, and I need to express it. We've tried to be private about it, because it's between me and Graham and because of you. I'm sorry that I didn't handle this better for your sake. But I thought you were beginning to like Graham. You seemed to."

Anthony shrugged. "I talked to him a few times, but that's all. I don't want him for my dad. I don't want anyone for my dad."

"Graham doesn't want to take your dad's place. Believe me, he doesn't." Tears blurred her eyes. "Anthony, how long are you going to punish yourself about Daddy? You didn't want to play baseball any longer, and that was okay. You were ten and you had so much on your plate with soccer too. You deserved to have some time for just being a kid. Daddy would have understood it, he did understand it, but he just thought you were so good that he didn't want you to lose your abilities. It's not fair to you that he didn't have the opportunity to tell you that. There will always be things left unsaid between people every single day, but Daddy knew you loved him. He knows it now." She took a deep breath. "He also knows he'll always be in a very special place in our hearts. But he's not here for either of us anymore. We've still got to live—"

"That's not going to make me like Graham."

Elaine stopped. She was pushing too hard, and maybe he was trying to justify his running away. "You don't have to like him. But, Anthony, don't run away anymore. Whatever problems we have here don't compare to out there. I was so scared that I'd lost you. I can't lose you."

Her hands were shaking when she grabbed him up and hugged him to her. To hell with adolescent aesthetics, she needed to know her son was safe and home. Anthony's arms came around her and he buried his face in her shoulder, just exactly as he did when he was a toddler and needed his mom.

Evidently he had said to hell with adolescent aesthetics too.

They both had a good cry.

Elaine swayed over Graham, her hips thrusting, pulling him deeply within her moist, velvety depths.

She was like a madwoman, he thought dimly as her hands pinned his over his head. Her breasts swayed enticingly just above his mouth. He captured one nipple and sucked hard, feeling the satiny nub extend into a throbbing point.

Elaine moaned. No one could hear her in his condo. No one but him. He felt the culmination of all his passion rise up within him, bursting forth to bathe her in his love. All his cares, all his troubles, even the world drained away as he renewed himself in her.

She shuddered, crying out his name and collapsing on top of him. "I love you, Graham. I love you so much."

He kissed her hair, though he could barely find the strength. "I love you."

They lay together, their arms wrapped around each other. He thought about these last weeks of chastity, ever since Anthony had run away. It seemed that the hotter the summer got, the cooler he and Elaine had become. At least intimately. In fact, they'd barely seen each other, because Elaine was afraid to leave Anthony alone. Graham

couldn't blame her. And he understood the need
for enforced abstinence because of the boy, although the whole situation worried and chafed
him. But Anthony was at his paternal grandparents'
for the weekend, and Elaine had taken advantage of
it to properly rejuvenate their relationship. He'd
needed this so badly. She must have, too, for she
had driven straight down from dropping Anthony
off.

Things were going right again . . . finally.

Neither of them made a move to get up for the
longest time, just enjoying the touch of skin to
skin. Her fragrance, warm and musky, filled his
senses. Occasionally he stroked her back from
shoulder to derriere. Her fingers sifted through the
hairs on his chest. Neither spoke. Graham had
never known such contentment. As far as he was
concerned, this could go on forever.

Eventually Elaine stirred, far too soon for him.
"I have to use the bathroom."

She slid away from him, taking her warmth
with her. The chill of the air conditioner drifted
across his skin, but he was too sapped of energy to
pull up the coverlet. He heard her pad toward the
bathroom, stop, then continue until the door
closed behind her. The click of the light switch
being turned on and the whir of the exhaust fan
barely registered in his dulled brain.

He must have slept, for he was suddenly aware
of the nightstand light blazing in his face. He
blinked and flinched away from its brightness, then

focused his eyes on Elaine standing next to the bed. She was fully dressed, her bag over one shoulder.

"I . . . we can't see each other anymore," she said.

"What?" He hadn't heard her right, he thought. He couldn't have.

"We can't see each other anymore," she repeated. Her face was a pale white in the light, while the rest of the room swirled like a surreal kaleidoscope behind her.

"I'm dreaming," he said in relief.

"No!" She grabbed his arm, and he could feel her nails digging almost painfully into his skin. "Graham. I can't! Anthony's running away and you don't want to hear about it! It's not working. It never was."

TWELVE

Graham scrambled out of bed, forcing Elaine back a step. He grabbed her arms, almost shaking her. "Elaine! What the hell are you talking about?"

"Us! Graham, face facts. We're not compatible where it counts. And I have a son who's very unhappy, and that means I have big problems. You're uncomfortable with children. You've said so before. I know you don't want my problems—"

"You can't do this," he said, his heart racing painfully with panic. "You've just hit a bad spell with Anthony—"

"This is more than a bad spell. I can't do it, Graham. I can't put all of us through the pain that's going to come if we continue."

"But you said you love me!"

"I do." Tears leaked out of the corners of her eyes. "I do. That's why I'm doing this."

"You're putting your son first. You're letting him rule you."

"He's not ruling me, but I have to put him first. And you." The tears flowed more freely. "I think we were just doomed from the start—"

"I won't let you do this!" he said, trying to pull her to him.

She jerked away. "I have to."

He followed behind her, trying to get to her before she reached the door. "Dammit, Elaine. You're not thinking straight—"

"Yes I am!" She began to run through his living room.

He closed in just as she reached the front door. He put his hand on it before she could open it. "Why did you come here tonight if we're so damned doomed like you think? Why did you make love with me? Why did you tell me you loved me?"

"Because I do!" she cried out. "Graham, please, don't make this worse than it is."

"You used me tonight. You used me all along."

"No!" The shock on her face was genuine, but it gave his pride no comfort. "How can you say such a thing?"

"This is a mistake, Elaine, letting Anthony run your life. I'm willing to work with Anthony, to wait him out until he accepts me. I know how he's feeling, even though it hurts a little. I've been there—"

"They're just words, Graham." Her expression changed to a more confident one. "When I tried to talk to you about Anthony's trouble at school, you were obviously uncomfortable—"

"No I wasn't!"

"Yes you were. And when he ran away, you wouldn't even come!"

"You *know* that's not true! How can you even say that? Elaine, be sensible—"

"I am. I have to put my son first out of necessity. He's only thirteen. Suppose we did get married . . . he would only get worse." She drew in a weepy breath. "Graham, I'm doing this for you most of all."

"Oh, no," he said. "You're not pulling that with me."

"Graham," she said wearily, "get dressed."

He gaped at her, confused by the shot from left field.

In that moment of his surprise, she got the door open. She walked through it and shut it with a soft finality.

Graham stared at the door. It had closed on a vital part of his life. His body was naked and vulnerable, but that was nothing compared to the wound in his heart.

John Kruk crushed the ball, hitting it into the upper deck of the stadium, a feat that had been accomplished by a handful of batters since the place opened nearly thirty years ago.

Elaine sat numbly in her seat as the people all

around her leaped up and cheered. She closed her eyes, not caring that her team had just gone ahead by a critical run in the eighth inning.

Her view was blocked anyway by the two men in front of her. She knew only one of them. Ed Tarksas had brought a client to the game. Her heart had nearly shot out of her body when she'd seen the advertising man come out of the concourse entrance below, but the man following Ed had been a stranger. A stranger in Graham's seat. She had no desire to spill her soda over this guy. Instead it had hurt so bad in her chest, she could barely breathe.

But she'd done what she'd had to do, breaking up with Graham. Nothing had ever hurt more. For the last two weeks she'd walked around like a zombie. She'd told Anthony of the breakup; he had been pleased and still was. She had wanted to wipe her son's smile off his face at the time. Even now she tried to tell herself not to be resentful because she had responsibilities to her child. Still, she couldn't help resenting those responsibilities. A few more years and Anthony would have been an adult . . . and she would have had no obstacles with Graham.

Graham had been right about one thing, though. She had used him that night. She'd only meant to go and explain why they could no longer see each other. But he'd grabbed her and kissed her breathless. She hadn't been able to stop herself from greedily making love one last time. He must hate her now.

"Are you all right, baby?"

Elaine opened her eyes to find Cleo practically leaning into her face. Jean and Mary were hovering behind her as best as they could in the aisle. All three wore expressions of concern.

She swallowed back a lump of tears. She had told them about the breakup shortly after it happened. She hadn't given details and she wasn't about to now. "I'm okay."

"You sure?"

She nodded, not trusting her voice.

They sat down, although all three were frowning. Anthony looked at her, then looked away. She had chosen son over man. It was a lonely choice she couldn't take back. But all her son's life she had stressed accepting one's responsibilities. Anthony was hers now.

She drew in a ragged breath, trying to compose herself. Tears leaked out of her eyes before she could stop them. She tried to catch them up, but sobbed instead. Cleo was instantly there, handing her a wad of tissues.

"Oh, Cleo," she wept, burying her face in the older woman's ample shoulder. She let out her tears with full force because she wasn't able to stop them.

"I've been expecting this," she heard Jean say.

"Well, what else could we expect?" Mary

chimed in, her beads clacking loudly. "She fell for him hard. We could all see that. I'll say a prayer."

"Prayers are only gonna help this baby so far," Cleo said. "A good cry's gonna help her more."

"Mom. Mom!"

Elaine turned her head. Through a veil of tears she saw Anthony's worried face. Even Ed Tarksas looked a little concerned.

"I'm okay," she lied, then burst into fresh tears.

Cleo rocked her. It was like being in her mother's embrace after skinning her knees as a child. "You just cry it out, honey. Ain't no man worth it, though."

"I did it. Not Graham. I loved him so much, and I did it."

Less than ten minutes later the Phillies won, and Elaine had never felt emptier.

She had done what she had to do.

Nearly October, Graham thought. Two months since he had last seen Elaine.

Paperwork surrounded him on his desk, but business wasn't the cure he'd thought it would be. He'd tried to hate her, but he couldn't. All that passion for her couldn't turn bad, would never turn bad. He couldn't stop the thoughts, though, the anger. That emotion hadn't diminished. She was making the same mistake his own mother made, giving in to a child. Maybe he had been a little uncomfortable with Anthony, but that didn't mean he didn't care. He had felt he had no right to comment about what she was doing with Anthony. Maybe he should have expressed more sympathy for her, but he was new at this and she should have recognized that. But she hadn't given him a chance.

Another thing he couldn't stop was the wanting. God, how he wanted her, needed her. Every day he bought a newspaper to check on the Phillies score, as if the game somehow kept him connected to her.

He sighed. He should have followed his first inclinations with her and kept away. Another lesson in life learned, as his mother would say. In fact, she'd had a lot to say when she'd heard about Elaine breaking off with him. Mostly that she felt sorry for them all.

Rubbing his hands over his face, he wished he could wash away ever meeting Elaine. Funny how things got repeated in life. His mother had given up her own life for him, and now Elaine was doing the exact same thing for her son.

He realized that he could go over and over and over this in his head and he would find no satisfaction at all. No relief from the pain. He pulled some computer printouts to him and forced himself to pay attention to the number crunching.

When the phone rang later, he surfaced in surprise, having actually been reading and comprehending the fiscal growth numbers for the next quarter. But after he answered the phone, the young voice on the other end nearly had him falling out of his leather chair.

"Anthony?" he asked tentatively, positive he was mishearing.

"This is Mr. Reed?"

"Yes. Anthony, why are you calling? Is everything all right? With you? With your mother?" Oh, Lord, he thought, his heart sinking past his stomach. Something had happened to Elaine.

"No, we're fine. I mean I am. But my mother isn't." The boy rushed on. "Well, she is. Okay, I mean, but she's not. She isn't sick or anything, not *sick* sick, but she's—"

"Anthony, slow down. Are you trying to say your mom's not ill, but something's happened? What's happened? Tell me slowly."

"Well, nothing's happened, I mean she's okay. Not sick or anything. She's just . . . not right."

"Not right?"

"Yeah. Not right. She cries a lot and she doesn't eat. Aunt Cleo says she's depressed. Aunt Mary's praying for her, and Aunt Jean says time heals all wounds but maybe not this time. I don't . . . I don't want my mom to be this way."

He felt the boy blaming him through the telephone line. "Anthony, I wouldn't have hurt your mother for the world. I loved her. But she didn't want to see me anymore. There's nothing I can do about that."

"Well, I thought maybe if you came to talk to

her . . . maybe if you told her you—you cared, maybe she'd feel better."

Graham tried to be gentle. "I could, but I don't think it would make a difference. You and I . . . well, we just didn't get along so well, and she was concerned about that. You haven't run away again or anything like that to cause your mother grief, have you?"

"No! That was dumb before. I know we . . . ahh, you're okay, I guess. It's just that I didn't think she liked you so much. And I thought things would be okay again if you weren't around. Like before. But they're not."

Graham realized the boy was trying to tell him he was willing to accept Graham in a relationship with his mother. Hope rose in his heart. It was a gutsy thing for the kid to call like this. Elaine had gone to great lengths to set examples for her son about the importance of accepting responsibility for one's actions. Here was the fruit of that labor . . . but it wasn't enough. "Anthony, your mother broke off with me because of you. I was very angry about that. I still am, especially because my mother gave up having a life for herself after my dad died. Did your mother ever tell you that my dad passed away when I was just a little younger than you are now?"

"No. I didn't know."

"I was twelve. I missed my father so much. Then I missed having a man to talk with about things. But my mom never went out with anybody.

Now all she has is one grown son who's busy with his own life. She has no one for her to care for or to care for her. I don't want that for your mom. I don't think you really do either."

"No." The child's voice was clear and strong.

Did he truly want what Anthony was offering? Even with the boy's cooperation, family life wouldn't be easy. Could he ever forgive Elaine for leaving him? Graham pressed Anthony further, wanting more assurance about the boy. "You know that if your mother and I were to start seeing each other again, I would be a part of your life. I wouldn't go away again just because you don't like me. I would be there permanently, forever. That is, if you and your mother will accept me."

There was silence over the line. "I know."

"I don't want to fight you at every turn either. No one can take your dad's place, and Lord knows I'm not equipped to even think of it. But I can be your friend. I want to be. And I think we make a pretty good pizza together. If you can't be friends with me, then say so now."

Graham waited. Anthony said nothing.

"I'm glad I've got a new friend," Graham said, smiling.

A sigh of relief whooshed out over the line.

"I'm very proud of you for calling me like this. It was a tough thing to do. You're a great kid, Anthony."

"Really?"

"Yes, really." Graham laughed in relief, then he

sobered. "You know your mom may not want me back—"

"Oh, she will. All she does is cry and mope."

Graham couldn't imagine Elaine in continual tears, yet his ego was thrilled with the news.

"Will you come?" Anthony asked. "Can you come now?"

Graham thought a moment. "I have a better idea."

The magic number was one. One more win and the Phillies would clinch the Eastern Division. If they won tonight, it wouldn't matter if every other National League East team won every one of their remaining regular season games and the Phillies lost every one of theirs. They would still be in first place and would move on to the National League play-offs, the last step to the World Series. And the best part was, they could do the magic number at home. Tonight.

The over 55,000 seats at the Vet were jam-packed with people bundled against the cool September night and filled with pennant fever. Almost jam-packed, Elaine thought. The seats in front of her were empty.

"You'd think Mr. Suit would have some big client to bring tonight," Cleo said, pointing to where Ed Tarksas usually sat.

"You'd think," Mary said disparagingly.

"Maybe Elaine could dump her soda on him too."

Anthony giggled. "Yeah, Mom. Maybe you'd get a boyfriend again."

Elaine turned and stared at her son, who suddenly sobered. "You all are in a good mood."

"Honey, where's your brain? This is the clincher tonight!" Cleo exclaimed. "We're going to the play-offs! It's been ten years since we been there. You remember?"

"I remember," Elaine said. She couldn't help smiling. Anthony had been a toddler, who'd fallen asleep in her arms amid all the pandemonium that year.

"We've sat through a lot of bad years since then," Jean said. "Mary, you got those beads going?"

"And ten lit candles at church, not to mention the novena I'm doing until they clinch."

"They'll probably clinch tomorrow in Pittsburgh," Elaine said, her moment of nostalgia gone and her depression returning.

"Shut up, Elaine," the three women chorused.

She sagged back in her chair, only half feeling the admonishment. Really, she shouldn't spoil their anticipation. But she couldn't muster any of her own.

What did she want anyway? If Graham were there, it would be sheer torture, and if someone else were in the seat, then that would be sheer torture too.

During the last few minutes before the game started, she saw Ed Tarksas emerge into the stadium amid the crush of people going in and out of the entrance. Her heart beat faster, even as she told herself he was bringing yet another *unknown* client to entertain at the game. She ought to know it wouldn't be Graham. He didn't even like baseball. Besides, either Tarksas had closed that advertising deal with Cove Pizzerias ages ago or Graham hadn't given it to him at all.

Graham came out of the concourse entrance behind Ed.

Elaine gasped. The world tilted sharply, like a sudden shift in a kaleidoscope. When she was able to focus again, she noticed he had a large cup of french fries and was eating one. She drank in his features, remembering all too well how his lips had tasted in a kiss. The men climbed the concrete stairs, and she stared at Graham the entire way up, not able to move her gaze in any other direction. She loved him so much, she'd let down every guard inside herself. And then she'd sent him away and gone back to her sterile life.

He glanced at her, then looked away. Her heart sank.

"Looks like Mr. Suit brought Mr. Suit," Cleo said, nudging Elaine.

"Maybe they got a thing for each other," Jean said.

"Maybe you got a sick mind," Mary told her crisply.

Anthony snorted.

"I feel sick," Elaine murmured as the scene before her swirled ominously.

"Go get your mamma a soda, baby," Cleo said to Anthony, handing over several dollar bills to the boy.

"Right."

Elaine watched as her son walked past the two men. He actually smiled at Graham, who smiled back. Both gestures were so surprising to her . . . and hurt so much that she couldn't stand it. "Now I know I'm sick."

The men made their way along their row to the empty seats in front of her. Graham greeted the three older women with charming words and an even more charming smile. Cleo, Jean, and Mary, the traitors, fawned over him. He didn't even look at Elaine before he sat down.

He hated her, she thought, feeling as though she'd been punched in the stomach. She couldn't blame him, but it hurt so much to see his blatant rejection. She looked down at his head and shoulders just an arm's reach away. If she shifted her feet forward a few inches, his back would be against her legs. So close and so unattainable.

She sat numbly in her molded plastic seat. Questions swirled through her mind. It never occurred to her that the three women she was with were oddly silent about the man in front of her. The most important game of the year, thus far, got underway. She only wanted to go home.

A soda cup was shoved in her hands. "Here, Mom."

Elaine glanced up and realized that Anthony had been away a long time, getting the soda. Anything could have happened to him, and she hadn't even considered his absence. "Anthony! Are you all right? You were gone a long time."

Her son made a face. "It took forever at the stand. There's a ton of people here, Mom."

Graham shifted in his seat, catching her attention. Of course, she thought. He was hearing her in full action over the reason she'd dumped him. She wanted so badly to apologize to him. She wanted so badly to ask him to take her back. But she couldn't, of course.

Somehow she sat through the first several innings, having no idea what was going on in the ball game. People around her cheered and groaned. Sometime during the fifth inning she glanced up at the electronic score strip on the other side of the stadium. The score was tied. The huge Panavision screen, called *Phanavision*, was showing scenes going on around the stadium. The Phillie Phanatic, a cross between an anteater and a moldy Big Bird, was in rare form as it cruised the aisles, kissing kids, stealing hats, and dancing with abandon. And Graham never turned around once, never made any gesture that indicated he was even aware of her behind him.

She began to wonder why he was there at all. He could have made any deal with Ed at an office.

He could have had any other kind of entertainment he'd wanted from the man. Tickets to the theater, a Rolling Stones concert, a basketball game, infinitely more preferable to him than a baseball game. So why was he there? To torture her, obviously. To throw in her face what she was missing.

Well, he was doing a damn good job of it.

Out of the corner of her eye she caught sight of the Phanatic and the Panavision cameraman making their way up her aisle. She realized that it was in between the fifth and sixth innings and they were scanning the crowd while the teams changed places and the pitcher warmed up on the mound. The huge green anteater/bird's goggly eyes looked so lifelike as they stared at her. They certainly weren't real, she knew that. But the damn thing was coming straight toward her!

The Phanatic began to make its way down her row, its big feet encased in size 100 high-tops. The creature squashed people back in their seats, sat on them, then dusted them off again. Everyone was laughing at its antics. She realized that Graham and Ed were standing, turning around toward her. At the top of the stadium, the *Phanavision* had her, *her*, on the enormous screen.

"Omigod!" she exclaimed, horrified at seeing herself, along with the 55,000-plus people at the stadium.

"Elaine," Graham said. "Elaine!"

She turned to him, feeling as if the world had just darkened and closed in on her.

"You'll either hate me or love me for this," he half shouted over the laughter. "But I can't stand being apart from you any longer. I love you. Will you marry me?"

She gaped at him, positive she hadn't heard him right. She became aware of Cleo and Jean and Mary giggling at her. Ed was grinning and looking smug. And Anthony, her Anthony, was laughing out loud at her. Although that could be because the Phanatic had its furry green arm around him.

"I don't want any half relationships anymore," Graham said, a sick look coming over his face at her silence. "I want to be in like a lion. Anthony's already said yes, so please, for all our sakes, will you marry me?"

"Don't leave the man standing there, baby," Cleo said, giving her a push. "Say something."

"Say something," Jean and Mary chorused.

Her dead brain clicked in and she realized this was a planned event. *Planned.* "Say something! Say something!"

"Yeah, Mom, say something," Anthony said, nudging her from the other side. "It's okay."

She looked at her son. "Anthony . . ."

He grinned and repeated, "It's *okay*, Mom."

The Phanatic nodded vigorously, its eyes bouncing in its head.

All kinds of emotions whirled through her like a lightning bolt. At last she said it the only way she knew how.

She dumped her soda over Graham's head.

Everyone gasped. Even the Phanatic made an appalled sound.

"Is this a yes?" Graham asked, soda running in dark sparkling rivulets down his suede jacket.

She grinned and fell into his arms. "Yes, you stinker! Yes!"

He kissed her soundly. "Thank God!"

A roar went up through the stadium.

"I'm sorry," she said as soon as she was able. "Oh, Graham, I'm so sorry."

"It's okay." He kissed her again. "We're together now. It's okay."

"I don't know how you did this, and I'll never forgive you for it," she murmured, kissing his cheeks. "But I love you."

She was grabbed out of Graham's arms, and a hot furry anteater mouth was smashed against her face. The Phanatic had kissed her. She got more-normal busses from Cleo, Jean, Mary, and even Ed. She was actually hugged by her son.

"Were you in on this?" she asked him.

The boy grinned. "Oh, yeah."

"I don't believe it." Tears sprang into her eyes. "And I don't understand, and I have lots of questions . . . but thank you."

Anthony hugged her again.

Graham took her gently back to him.

"You have got a lot of explaining to do," she said.

"And you've got a cleaning bill to pay. Again." He laughed. "I love you."

"I love you." One question couldn't wait. "How did you do this?"

"Anthony, the girls, and Ed. He got it on the television. I figured you wouldn't say no in front of a stadium full of people." He chuckled. "I didn't think you'd chuck your soda at me, though."

"How else would I say yes?" She pulled Anthony in with them. "I love you so much."

"Group hug!" Cleo shouted.

The Widows' Club joined in. Even Ed got in. And all of them were enfolded in the huge furry green arms of the Phanatic.

Elaine had never been happier in her life, and she didn't even care that the Phillies lost later on.

But they clinched in Pittsburgh.

The wedding had to wait until after the World Series.

"Did it have to go to seven games?" Graham asked, after paying off the bellman on their wedding night.

"What more could you ask for in the way of excitement?" Elaine said. She slipped off her cream-colored satin pumps and fell into a plush armchair in the living room of the Bellevue Hotel's best suite. "A loss . . . a win . . . another loss at home . . . a 15–14 hitter's dream of a game which we lost in the bottom half of the *ninth* inning . . . a beautifully pitched shutout by Curt Schilling to win the fifth and stay alive . . . a scrambling win for game six . . . and Danny Jackson blowing those stinking Blue Jays away to win game seven and the World Series."

"Where we almost got killed when you four women went nuts in that crowd of Jays fans," he reminded her as he sat down on the arm of her chair. "You even got my mother going! I think she's taking your place in the Widows' Club."

"I think so too. Those three will shape her up." She reached up and cupped his face, bringing him down for a lingering kiss. "Now quit complaining about all the excitement. It's got me *very* revved up for my wedding night. Like Cleo, I have all this excitement to work off. World Series excitement."

"I think it was the big green hairy thing." He slid into the seat next to her, deftly shifting her onto his lap.

"I must admit you took me by surprise with your method of proposal," she murmured. "I still can't believe Anthony called you like that."

"He's some kid you've got there. *We've* got there." He slipped open the buttons on the jacket of her cream silk suit. She had looked positively beautiful at their small wedding of family and friends, but now he wanted her in her most beautiful state. Naked. "I think I'm getting the hang of this kid thing. Can we make some more?"

"Oh, absolutely."

"Truly?" he asked, realizing a whole unknown stretched ahead of them. But it was an unknown he wanted so badly, filled with love and laughter. "Do you think I'll be all right?"

She smiled and fiddled with the buttons of his shirt. "I think you'll be wonderful. Watch and see."

He did.

THE EDITOR'S CORNER

Along with May flowers come four terrific new LOVESWEPTs that will dazzle you with humor, excitement, and passion. Reading the best romances from the finest authors—what better way to enjoy the beauty and magic of spring?

Starting things off is the fabulous Mary Kay McComas with a love story that is the **TALK OF THE TOWN**, LOVESWEPT #738. Rosemary Wickum always finds some wonderful treasures in the refuse center, pieces perfect for her metal sculptures, but one thing she never goes looking for is a man! When recycling whiz Gary Albright begins pursuing her with shameless persistence, everyone in town starts rooting for romance. Once he nurses the embers of her passion back to life, he must convince his lady he'll always warm her heart. Irresistible characters and frisky humor make this latest Mary Kay story a tenderhearted treat—and proves that love can find us in the most unlikely places.

From the delightful Elaine Lakso comes another winner with **TASTING TROUBLE**, LOVE-SWEPT #739. Joshua Farrington doesn't think much of the Lakeview Restaurant's food or ambience, but its owner Liss Harding whets his interest and provokes him into a brash charade! Tempting her with strawberries, kissing her in the wine cellar, Josh coaxes her to renovate the building, update the menu —and lose herself in his arms. But once he confesses his identity, he has to persuade her he isn't the enemy. As delectable as chocolate, as intoxicating as fine wine, this wonderful romance from Elaine introduces charming, complex lovers whose dreams are more alike than they can imagine.

From the ever-popular Erica Spindler comes **SLOW HEAT**, LOVESWEPT #740. Jack Jacobs thrives on excitement, thrills to a challenge, and always plays to win, so when the sexy TV film critic is teamed with Jill Lansing, he expects fireworks! Five years before, they'd been wildly, recklessly in love, but he couldn't give her the promise she'd craved. Now she needs a hero, a man who'll share his soul at last. He is her destiny, her perfect partner in work and in bed, but can Jill make him understand he has to fight for what he wants—and that her love is worth fighting for? Steamy with innuendo, sparkling with wit, Erica's exhilarating battle of the sexes reunites a fiery pair of lovers—and casts an enchanting spell!

Rising star Maris Soule offers a hero who is full of **DARK TEMPTATION**, LOVESWEPT #741. Did special-effects genius Jason McLain really murder his wife, as the tabloids claimed? Valerie Wiggins approaches his spooky old house, hoping to convince him to help her make their Halloween charity event truly frightening. But when he opens the door, her heart races not with fright but sizzling arousal. Jason fears caring for Val will put her in danger, but maybe helping her face her demons will silence his own. Torn by doubts, burning with desire, can a man and a woman who'd first touched in darkness find themselves healed by the dawn? In a heartstopping novel of passion and suspense, Maris explores our deepest terrors and most poignant longings in the journey that transforms strangers into soulmates.

Happy reading!

With warmest wishes,

Beth de Guzman
Senior Editor

Shauna Summers
Associate Editor

P.S. Don't miss the women's novels coming your way in May: **DARK RIDER** from *The New York Times* bestselling author Iris Johansen is an electrifying tale of deadly and forbidden desire that sweeps from the exotic islands of a tropical paradise to the magnificent estates of Regency England; **LOVE STORM** by Susan Johnson, the bestselling mistress of the erotic historical romance, is the legendary, long out-of-print novel of tempestuous passion; **PROMISE ME MAGIC** by the extraordinary Patricia Camden is a "Once Upon a Time" historical romance of passion and adventure in the tradition of Laura Kinsale. And immediately following this page, look for a preview of the exciting romances from Bantam that are *available now!*

Don't miss these extraordinary books
by your favorite Bantam authors

On sale in March:

MISTRESS
by Amanda Quick

DANGEROUS TO KISS
by Elizabeth Thornton

LONG NIGHT MOON
by Theresa Weir

DANGEROUS
TO KISS
by Elizabeth Thornton

"A major, major talent . . . a genre superstar."
—*Rave Reviews*

Handsome, kind, and unassuming, Mr. Gray seemed the answer to Deborah Weyman's prayers. For once she accepted the position he offered, she would finally be safe from the notorious Lord Kendal, a man she had good reason to believe had murdered her former employer—and was now after her. But there were certain things about Mr. Gray that Deborah should have noticed: the breadth of his shoulders, the steel in his voice, the gleam in his uncommonly blue eyes—things that might have warned her that Mr. Gray was no savior but a very dangerous man. . . .

"Study hall," said Deborah brightly, addressing Mr. Gray, and all the girls groaned.

With a few muttered protests and a great deal of snickering, the girls began to file out of the room. Deborah assisted their progress by holding the door for them, reminding them cheerfully that on the morrow they would be reviewing irregular French verbs and she expected them to have mastered their conjugations. As the last girl slipped by her, Deborah shut the door with a snap, then rested her back against it, taking a moment or two to collect herself.

Suddenly aware that Mr. Gray had risen at their exit and was standing awkwardly by the window, she politely invited him to be seated. "You'll have a glass of sherry?" she inquired. At Miss Hare's, the guests were invariably treated to a glass of sherry when the ordeal of taking tea was over. At his nod, Deborah moved to the sideboard against the wall. The glasses and decanter were concealed behind a locked door, and she had to stoop to retrieve them from their hiding place.

As he seated himself, Gray's gaze wandered over the lush curves of her bottom. There was an appreciative glint in his eye. The thought that was going through his head was that Deborah Weyman bore no resemblance to the descriptions he had been given of her. Spinsterish? Straitlaced? Dull and uninteresting? That's what she wanted people to think. She had certainly dressed for the part with her high-necked, long-sleeved blue kerseymere and the ubiquitous white mobcap pulled down to cover her hair. An untrained eye would look no further. Unhappily for the lady, not only was he a trained observer, but he was also an acknowledged connoisseur of women. Advantage to him.

Since her attention was riveted on the two glasses of sherry on the tray she was carrying, he took the liberty of studying her at leisure. Her complexion was tinged with gray—powder, he presumed—in an attempt to add years and dignity to sculpted bones that accredited beauties of the *ton* would kill for. The shapeless gown served her no better than the gray face powder. She had the kind of figure that would look good in the current high-waisted diaphanous